Congrats.

Enjoy Nauhu!

CALL OF THE
STORM SORCERER

The Serpentine Throne Book One

Susan Stradiotto

BRONZEWOOD
BOOKS

Eden Prairie, MN

CALL OF THE STORM SORCERER

© 2021 Susan Stradiotto

Published by
Bronzewood Books
14920 Ironwood Ct.
Eden Prairie, MN 55346

Cover & Interior Design: Bronzewood Books

Edited by: Owl Pro Editing

Library of Congress Control Number: 2020924755

Paperback ISBN-13: 978-1-949357-19-6

eBook ISBN-13: 978-1-949357-18-9

Printed in USA

Dedicated to:

*My wonderfully imaginative son Keeton
Stradiotto for inspiring such an adventure
through a steadfast love of all things dragon.*

THE NOR┊
BARR┊

TAMATORI

THE SYRENSEA

ISE

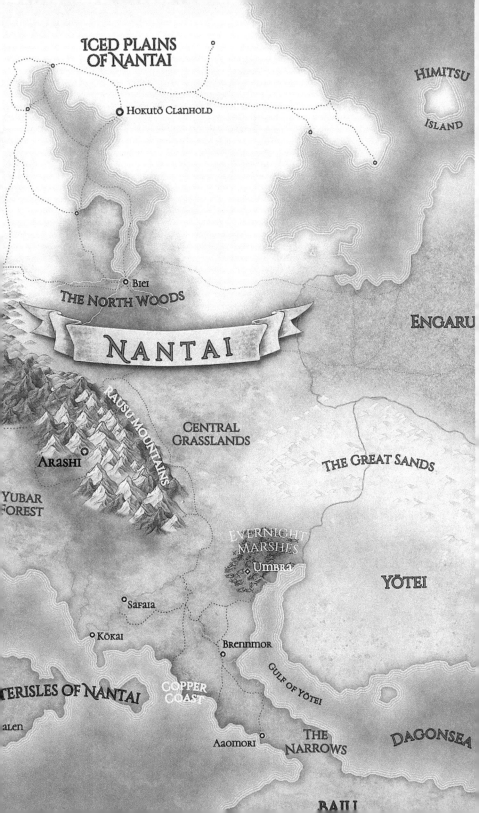

MAKENYN
Emperor of Nantai

HE HID IN DARKNESS, squeezing his eyes ever tighter in an effort to shutter his mind from the voice, to armor his heart from the feelings of otherness bound to his soul.

This plan you've written will bring you no peace, the voice inside rumbled as loudly as if someone other than he could hear, as deeply as thunder.

Makenyn could call the clouds and thunder to shield himself from the presence and sound were he outside, if only he had access to the elements. Instead, he chanted, "No, no, no," and curled tighter into himself. Within the jewel city of Arashi, his mental intruder had reduced him to a cowering man alone in a black cave beneath his beloved Stormskeep. Makenyn, ascended emperor of the Nantai people and first within the elite caste—the Storm Sorcerers—rocked back and forth on the balls of his feet, his legs bent, chest pressed tight to his knees, head down, and hands covering his ears. He wailed, "Stay out of my head and heart!"

He'd chosen the cavern for its absence of windows and had had a door installed to further block out any light. The measures deprived his senses and restricted his sorcery, but that was the price he willingly paid to silence the beast within. Seclusion and darkness had worked for a time, and the Ryū dragon had slept until he grew hungry and sensed his prison. As he stirred again within, Makenyn could feel Kuroi's nerves thrumming under his own skin, trying to escape. He stood, gritted his teeth, clenched his fists, and fought the heat rising in his blood and the prickle across his skin where scales threatened to erupt.

He would not shift.

He threw his head back and yelled, "No!" into the darkness, his voice coming back to his ears over and over again until it silenced. "I won't let it happen again. I cannot."

Makenyn, answer unto me. Why do you wish this thing? the fiend bellowed. *It will break us both.*

"Leave me, you accursed spirit!" Makenyn growled through his teeth, spittle wetting his chin.

This is not the way, minikin—

"DO NOT call me that!" The emperor's voice echoed again as the door crept inward.

"Pardon, Tennō?" a timid yet familiar voice asked, using Makenyn's honorary title even though the two were related.

"Morwyn," he breathed, panted. "Come, Brother. And close the door behind you."

Light beamed into the room, and Makenyn squinted against its burn. He paused, listening and feeling, then breathed with relief that Kuroi had retreated to someplace deeper inside . . . if only for a time.

Morwyn's feet shuffled against the floor, his steps less sure than the emperor's who'd learned every knot and bump on every stone within the room over time.

Makenyn paced, demanding, "Is the separation ritual prepared?"

"Yes, Tennō. Nityn awaits you now. I've brought material for your eyes if you'll find me here in the dark. Then I will guide you to the chamber he has readied."

Though this was the right path—the only path toward seeing himself whole once again—the emperor paused.

"Tennō Makenyn?" Morwyn asked.

"Yes, yes." He rubbed a hand over his beard, the whiskers no longer bristling under the touch as they'd grown long enough in the darkness to become soft. Aloud, but not directed at Morwyn in truth, he mused, "So, the time has come at last."

"Yes, Tennō. I have prepared everything as you wished."

Makenyn took a deep breath and closed his eyes as he exhaled slowly. Though he might perish in the casting by the shaman who'd separate him from the Ryū dragon within, he felt a certain peace—a sense of rightness in his decision. Yet two things gave him pause, tempting him to reconsider. He'd held himself in darkness for so long, only allowing the tiniest of flame on occasion to pen a decree, and his brother would be a weak ruler for the Nantai people while he recovered. Morwyn had been his mouthpiece for some number of moons. How many, the emperor couldn't count, but Morwyn remained little more than a puppet for Makenyn's decrees. No one person across Nantai could speak to the results of the impending ritual, for none before had dared attempt to sever the soul-deep bond between a person and his Ryū dragon.

I beg of you, minikin, do not go through with this ritual, Kuroi said.

Hissing, Makenyn pressed his palms to his ears as if he could block the sound. Pointless. It came from inside.

He walked to his brother, only needing the sound of his breathing to locate his position. "Give me the material. I am ready."

Morwyn made no reply, but the emperor found his fumbling hands and took the length of fabric, deftly folding it on the diagonal.

"Tennō Makenyn, if I may?"

In the darkness, the emperor could hear the slight rasp where his brother twisted and wrung his hands—the ever-present nerves and uncertainty that made him a poor fit for emperor of the Nantai people. Makenyn sucked in a sharp breath as he secured the fold about his eyes. "What is it, Brother?"

"A-are you certain of this? The green dragon—"

"Guin?" the emperor prompted, surprise riddling his mind. Why would Morwyn mention her, Kuroi's mate?

"Yes. Since you have been in isolation, the green dragon has been circling over Arashi and the keep almost daily. She is a frightful Ryū, and our people shrink and hide in their homes, fearing her wrath. Have you not heard her cries, Tennō?"

This deep within the belly of Stormskeep, insulated

by the mountain and the castle's foundation, he heard none of the sounds from above. Indeed, he had longed for the normal sounds—servants bustling about or the sound of the Sundai Falls and the feel of their mists upon his face as he stood upon his terrace. Resolved, he answered, "Morwyn, that I have not heard things from above in uncountable months, that I have not been a citizen of my own empire, and that this presence inside me refuses to leave me in peace . . . those are all reasons why I have commanded Nityn to complete this ritual." Makenyn took a deep breath, his shoulders expanding and contracting. "Then the beasts can leave Stormskeep and the city of Arashi, and hopefully Nantai itself, together. You see, I am giving them what they want."

That is not how it will work, the beast grumbled.

"What do you know?" Makenyn roared.

Morwyn shuffled away at the sound.

The emperor sighed, attempting to gather himself. Of course, all his brother had heard was Makenyn's reaction. He inhaled and sighed again. "You see, Brother, I must do this thing to rid my soul of its ghosts. Now, you will take me to Nityn." He moved closer to his brother, taking hold of Morwyn's elbow and leading him to the door, the end of his dark domain.

The walk was a journey of three hundred eighty-seven paces, two dozen spiral stone steps, and another seventy-two paces to the chambers Nityn had prepared. Morwyn trembled the entire time under Makenyn's grip. As they entered, smoky smells of herbs burning in a fire and hearty smells of something brewing wafted through the air. The small sound of liquid bubbling reached Makenyn's ears, and it felt tepid and sticky inside. "Is it dark enough, Brother?" he asked, hesitant to remove the material from his eyes.

"Yes." Morwyn's arm slipped from his grip.

With eyes uncovered, he took in the room with sight and sound, musing over the connection between the two senses. Upon the far wall, a large opening lay hidden by layers of heavy material to shut out most of the light. It worked but for a bright line on either side. Makenyn averted his eyes from those points as the brightness stung, but knowing of the opening behind the drape, he listened too. So near the Sundai Falls, the sound of rushing water soothed his soul for long moments—a sight he longed to behold again, waters he wished to call upon with his own storm sorcery and stir forth a shower that would wash away the darkness and grime. The time would come. One day soon, he'd no longer be a prisoner to this evil within.

Nityn awaited behind a waist-high stone slab. A Storm Sorcerer who'd adopted shamanism and studied spellcasting in relation to ritualistic magics for years, Nityn would be the savior of all Makenyn held close, the one to separate the Ryū dragon from Makenyn's soul. Black robes hung upon Nityn's narrow shoulders, every one of his features thin and angular. Even the shape of his brows, mustache, and black beard emphasized the sharp slants of his cheekbones and jaws. He spread his arms, the robes falling like crow's wings, then lay his twig-like fingers upon the stone. "My tennō, you will disrobe and lay here upon your stomach."

A shriek sounded outside the cavern's hidden opening, and all three men jumped. Makenyn's blood and skin heated in reply, and he had to lock down his muscles to control the shift. With his eyes closed and through clenched teeth, he said, "Soon, Ryū. Soon you will be free to go with her." He refused to voice the evil spirit's name.

Inside, the grumble came again, *This is madness, minikin. This will not work as you desire. I warn you of that.*

Makenyn's eyes flew open and he looked about the chambers wildly. The others hadn't heard the gravelly voice, only his. The emperor snapped, "We must begin. Morwyn, are you ready with your oaths?" He must be certain things were in order.

"Yes, Tennō. And the High Cloud Court is due to arrive on the morrow so I may ascend and tend to matters of the realm whilst you recover." Morwyn's brows pinched together, holding his worry tight upon his forehead. As the man had been born of the same mother and father, he resembled the image Makenyn recalled of himself in the mirror, but Morwyn also seemed meeker.

The emperor said a quick prayer to the Triad that his recovery would be swift, that he'd be fit to rule in a short time. With a nod, he removed his clothes. Nityn offered him a bowl with a green-tinged liquid. Makenyn quirked a brow.

"The potion will calm you, keep you still, and lessen the pain, my tennō." Nityn's features portrayed naught of what he possibly thought in the moment.

Though he accepted the bowl, Makenyn said, "I have commissioned you well, Nityn. I trust that this is no poison?"

"Tennō, with respect due to you as emperor, I am not to receive the second half of my commission until I successfully perform this task. Furthermore, if you die in the process, my fate is likewise death. You have offered sufficient incentive to see to your health and longevity, Tennō." He bowed his head then—stiffly.

Makenyn drank, the putrid liquid poorly disguised by bee's nectar, and climbed onto the stone slab. Despite the heat and humidity that hung about, the stone felt cool. Shivers ran through his body as he lowered his feverish skin onto the rock. When he rested flat upon his stomach, he felt cooler on the front than he could recall since bonding with the Ryū, yet the skin upon his back was still ablaze. Still within the emperor's sight, Nityn meandered about the room, collecting a knife, some wicked hinged device, and bowls. He gathered coals from the fire inside an enormous stone bowl, and the knife tinkled when he placed it inside. While the blade heated, he cleared the sizable area in front of the heavy curtains—presumably where the Ryū would rest in dragon form after the ritual, the long-awaited moment when Makenyn and Kuroidragon were once again individuals.

A haze settled over Makenyn as Morwyn stepped close to his head.

"Brother," he whispered in the familiar, a catch to his voice, "I will be right here with you for the duration. In that corner there where you may see me. And until you heal, I will see to your empire."

Makenyn's eyes drifted closed, then slowly open again, and his lips felt numb. Inside, Kuroi's soul felt heavy, too, but with melancholy rather than potion. That was well enough; it would all be over soon.

Nityn chanted, incomprehensible incantations and likely an invocation of some ill deity he'd found to aide in the ritual. Though Nityn had assured Makenyn the ritual would achieve his ultimate desire, he'd wished to know little of the workings. Nityn had warned of the pain, but the emperor considered that temporary, a fair price to be alone within his mind and body once again.

"All is prepared," Nityn said, the words seeming distant and slurred. "I must create the exit along the spine. The potion will hold you still, but I fear you must endure the pain awake."

Makenyn tried to nod, but his body was indeed immobile. He marveled over the feeling. Everything seemed like a smoke dream, yet he remained aware. Nityn reached for the knife resting in the coals. The blade glowed. The shaman moved behind him, out of sight. Then nothing happened for what felt an eternity until . . .

Sharp, hot, severing pain descended at the base of his neck. Makenyn tried to scream. Nothing. The pain traced down his back. Sizzling reached his ears. His mind told him to flee. Nothing. The smell of roasting flesh filled his nose. The searing moved between his shoulders, along his spine. Nityn hissed and there was more pressure in the center of his back. Makenyn could do naught but endure. More sizzling. Stronger odors. Pain again, moving down his lower back and all the way to his tailbone. The motion stopped, his back pulsing in agony, his soul wanting to cry to the heavens, but his body frozen.

"I've completed the first step," breathed Nityn. As he took the knife back to the coals and placed the bloodied blade inside, he murmured more foreign words.

Makenyn wanted to cry, breathe heavier, anything, but the potion regulated everything. Every involuntary action continued at a fixed tempo. His back pulsed, and the sound of metal clashing and ringing filled his ears, though he thought that only inside. Nityn lifted the hinged thing and once again moved out of sight. Had he control, Makenyn would gasp in fear, shock. Yet his body wouldn't listen to his urges. At the center of his back, he felt pressure and something sliding inside, gripping at his spine. A peal sounded from the instrument and his back separated. Crackling came where ribs parted from spine, and his body rounded forward by force.

Nityn chanted.

Metal clanged.

Morwyn, in the corner's shadows, bent and retched.

And Makenyn lay utterly still, his back split from neck to tailbone, his body arching from the stone as a force beyond reckon pulled at his soul.

Nityn chanted, volume growing above the din with every exotic word.

Everything screeched, twisted, echoed, pulled, pounded, and writhed.

Until his mind could withstand the torment no more.

The Fifth Age

Princess Mairynne Evangale

ONE

Nantai in Mourning

GENERATIONS HAVE PASSED SINCE the Ryū Wars, the age when the great dragons and people split and became mortal foes. Yet the Nantai people, my people, remain. I have never met one of the Ryū, the dragons of old, nor have I felt the ties of companionship, but our people's lessons were ingrained. The Ryū bond represented the purest variety of evil. From before I gained knowledge of letters, my sisters and I clung to stories Father had told. Karynne, Yasmynne, and I had gathered at his feet near the throne crafted from the last dragon's skin and bone and scale, and we listened to Tennō Atheryn read from Stormskeep's annals. His voice had resonated in my blood as he'd painted the history of companionship, the most toxic of bonds between a dragon and a person.

The stories had been as exciting as they were dangerous. During the time at my father's heel, I'd been too young to understand or wield my storm sorcery with any bit of control, but my sisters would stir small gusts of wind, animating dyed sands to enact the scenes. Between Father's booming narration and the miniature scenes, I'd giggle and clap and thoroughly enjoy the show.

Over the course of the histories read, it became clear that the Ryū bond drove people to commit acts unimaginable. Father wouldn't read to us of the treachery, but he did share one story—a story that kept me awake in the dark hours for many moons, the story of the people's first emperor: Tennō Makenyn, the Scarred. After surviving the ritual that peeled away the soul-deep bond between him and the blackest dragon, Kuroidragon, he wore the scars for the remainder of his days and walked hunchbacked, limping as he went.

I closed and reopened my eyes slowly, returning to my chambers, to the now, and to myself, my shoulders laden under the weight of both the memory and the mourning robes my attendants were draping about my shoulders. The material well-positioned, Mother Feathergale scurried to the adjacent room to retrieve the lengths of fabric that would secure the garments and further restrict my ability to breathe easily. Desperate to put away the heavy garments prescribed for the sixty days and nights of mourning my father had declared in the wake of my mother's death, I asked, "How many more?" I'd asked the same question every morn as they attended to my attire.

Yet my friend and attendant answered readily, "A dozen days remain, Lady Mairynne." Jessa bobbed in deference to my impending position.

I clasped her shoulders and waited for her gaze to

lift, to meet mine, then said, "Please don't treat me so. I'm the same person I was ten days ago before Tennō Atheryn Evangale went missing, and I'll be the same person tomorrow and after this period of mourning has passed."

"Yes, Lady Mairy—"

I squeezed to silence her formal objection. Looking sternly into her worried eyes, I said, "Simply Mairynne. The same Mairynne who has been at your side since we were younglings." When her tension eased, mine did the same. I gulped air, rolling my shoulders back to support the robes' weight.

Employed by my parents to care for their royal children and known to us as Mother Feathergale, Jessa's blooded mother returned to my chambers. She looked small in comparison to the swaths of belting material overflowing her grasp, but it didn't appear a burden. She used her sorcery, stirred a minor wind to carry the heavy belts, and she simply guided them toward the bed. I released my dear friend and turned to face the mirror. The royal mourning garments were extensive, so Jessa went to help. As they returned, I lifted my arms to receive the finishing touches.

To my attendants and to the Holy Triad should they be listening, I raised my chin and voice. "How are the city's people handling the loss? And the people beyond?"

Mother Feathergale revolved around me, binding my body with the blessed robes so I might feel embraced by my loved one lost. She worked proficiently and spoke with a cutting absence when she answered, "They await patiently, per tradition. And you shouldn't toil over the matter now. The Triad intends for you to focus on healing during the quiet time. Decreed by the blessed emperor and respected by all castes and the casteless alike."

In the long days while I waited idly, and more so within that moment, I felt inclined to curse the traditions, shun the robes, and escape the stony walls that bound me to the castle and citadel. I longed for action, to discover if others believed—as did I—that Father still lived. I yearned to see how the people were reacting to the loss of both their rulers. Still working to gain necessary confidence in my convictions, I spoke more quietly, with uncertainty, and voiced words that I dared not speak to anyone less trusted than Jessa and Mother Feathergale, "With all that has happened, do you not believe the rituals selfish at all?"

Mother Feathergale finished securing the ends of the obi and came to face me, her eyes blinking, then widening with bewilderment. "Why ever would it be selfish, Mairynne?"

Lowering my eyes, I smiled ruefully. Had I truly expected her to hold beliefs outside of those handed down for generations?

My aging attendant wiped her palms on her apron and opened her arms to me with a smile. I fell willingly into her embrace as she offered me what comfort she could, but in the end, she pushed me away with a solemn look, misty eyes, and slight nod. "There, you're ready for the day. Your mother would be proud. Your father too," she added.

I swallowed against the sudden burn in my throat. Her gaze left mine as she inspected the belts, making tiny adjustments while I, too, gathered myself. I would not cry. I'd done enough of that since my mother's death. For my father to have disappeared so soon after, I felt cracked, as if a fissure ran through my soul. The realm seemed to feel the same, and the recovery of a people who had lost their leaders lurked in the wings as everyone respected one of our most sacred beliefs and waited for the rites of mourning to pass. While I loathed the clothing and sense of confinement, I also dreaded the completion of the sixty days and nights and the duty that awaited once mourning had passed.

I picked up my skirts and lumbered toward the door.

"Mairynne," Mother Feathergale called, "we still need to bind your hair."

Pushing my chin higher, I said, "I think I'll leave it loose."

"But—"

I held a hand forward to halt the propriety. I would wear the clothing, but I refused the hair. Finishing my day with a headache from the constant pull was the last of my desires. Traditionally, the decision may have been blasphemous, but there were no formal ceremonies this day. Outside of going to the citadel, I wouldn't meet any of my people. My sisters and the Triad's priests could tolerate my small defiance.

The older woman clasped her hands and put on a smile. "You have always been a headstrong child. Your mother and I have always been there to encourage your determination." She curtsied. "As you will."

To my friend, I asked, "Jessa, will you walk with me?"

She lifted her own robes of mourning, although significantly less encumbering than mine, and joined me at the door. I envied her for her lack of station, but I'd little choice as to my own. These walls held me as did the propriety and custom. The robes simply ensured I couldn't breathe.

Before leaving, I turned. "Thank you, Mother

Feathergale. For everything."

Despite my sense of suffocation, I'd been fortunate to have gained my majority having two motherly figures in my life—my best friend's mother and the woman who had borne my sisters and me into the world. Before her death, Noralynne Evangale had possessed strength and compassion revered by all castes of our people. Nantai's casteless and Small Folk had also loved the empress, a fondness rulers before her couldn't claim. As I turned down the hall toward the bridge, I grasped the two small tokens that hung on a chain around my neck; one stone felt constantly warm against my skin and the other constantly cold. The soldiers who found Mother had pulled the cold thing from her hand after recovering her twisted body from the border of the Evernight Marshes near the Great Sands. The warm stone I had found on my father's pillow the morning he, Tennō Atheryn Evangale, had disappeared.

◇◇◇◇◇◇◇◇◇◇◇◇◇◇◇◇

WITHIN NANTAI'S JEWEL CITY of Arashi, Stormskeep Castle hugged the side of a cliff high above a great waterfall. We exited the castle proper onto a wide landing, then moved toward the bridge crossing high above Sundai Falls. Our steps carried us onward over the narrow bridge to the citadel beyond where my sisters and I would meet with priests and receive updates on the upcoming rites. Though I'd grown up in the people's central city, I had no memories at Stormskeep in which the sound of water flowing over stone did not provide ambiance. Even in the most remote corners of the castle, if I were to listen, I could have heard the wooshing and splashes. Now, as we slowly crossed the bridge over the falls, the ever-present sound soothed my nerves.

Each tentative foot forward caused the bridge to

sway, and I questioned my balance. Should I fall, I could call the wind to carry me to safety, but it would incite commotion and angst over my well-being amongst any people gathered below in the daylight hours. Today, I wished for privacy, and the need to face my sisters as well as the Triad was burden enough, so I took care and held the rough rope railing as I walked shoulder-to-shoulder with Jessa. She, on the other hand, moved freely in her light-weight robes.

Again, I envied her.

"You seem distant today," Jessa said, turning to face me then quickly back to our path.

I breathed deeply and sighed. "My mind is clouded with what's needed to complete the rituals. Day forty-eight, you said?"

"Mmm, yes."

"We only have three rites remaining and then we can dispense with the sadness that hangs over our people."

"Over your people, Lady Mairynne. Afterward, do you intend to prepare for ascension?"

I stopped both walking and breathing, but my question spilled out anyway. "Why would you ask such a question so carelessly?" I said, scanning for onlookers.

She fumbled to find decorum and the right response. "My apologies, Lady Mairynne. I just figured we were alone and that the sounds of the falls would mask the question."

I had wounded her. For her to have asked only reflected my own worry; I had scolded where I should not have. "No, Jessa, it is I who should apologize. My ascension is the expectation of the people, is it not?" Truly, this was no answer, but I hoped it was enough to appease her curiosity.

It sufficed. She eased, looped an arm through mine, and offered her strength to supplement my own.

Halfway across the bridge, I stopped and turned to face the falls. Mist wafted up on the wind from the rocks, cooling my face and stirring my loose hair. To my oldest friend, I said, "If—and that is a big if—I do, I've much to prepare over the next twelve days. I'm not ready to be empress, and I fear I am not truly ready for the burden."

"Mairynne, there is reason—"

"I know the reason behind all of this." Shaking my head, I grasped her hand and eased my words for her benefit. "My parents groomed me, along with my sisters, for this very thing, but the time came far sooner than I had thought." I paused, looking down at our clasped hands. "They, my parents, that is, were taken from us before their time."

Jessa hugged me around the shoulders, her simple touch, silence, and acceptance offering more strength than she knew.

"Anyway," I said at last and a mite ruefully, "my remaining family awaits my arrival. We'd best be on our way."

Inside the citadel, we turned to the right and made for the Triad's meeting chambers behind the temple proper. At a long table, the Triad's clergy sat in chairs in a seemingly random pattern, each reading from a scroll. My sisters and their first advisors also awaited. Karynne sat at the table's head, and I wondered how early she'd arrived to secure the seat of power. To her left, Yasmynne leaned close to her betrothed, Nestryn.

Upon my father's disappearance, my sisters had

wasted no time in choosing and announcing their first advisors. The thought caused my stomach to churn. Nestryn had now been elevated to Yasmynne's first advisor, yet they sat too close, too intimately for an official proceeding. Their manner had always been an open display of affection, and they paid little heed to the company present. Poised behind Karynne, the powerful, more seductive Imrythel Sandsgale rested one hand on the back of my sister's chair. She, Karynne's chosen, was almost too much to behold, ebony hair flowing, one eye covered with a black veil while the other peered back, an uncommonly piercing green. Merely looking upon her, I felt out of place in my own skin and fought the urge to fidget.

Wearing attire that mirrored my own, Karynne stood and closed the distance between us. Having our father's height, she looked down, grasped my shoulders, and folded me into a hug. "Mairynne," she said. "How are you doing this morning?"

"I do wish we didn't have to do this today," I answered. "But if we must, let us begin."

Karynne's glance flickered past me to Jessa but returned quickly, and with a smile, she nudged me toward the chair at her right. "Sister, why is your hair unbound?"

Yasmynne surfaced from her whispers and flipped a hand in their oldest sister's direction. "Oh Kahry, let her be. This is our only obligation today."

Across the table, I gave Yasmynne a thankful but questioning stare.

The elderly priest cleared his throat and rolled up his scroll. "With you all here, we may proceed."

The other clergy, each given the Hallowgale name by tradition and raised to serve the Triad, followed his lead in stowing their reading.

The much younger priestess said, "Edamyn, we should excuse the advisors." The notes in Tasmynne's voice rang high and clear as she looked meaningfully from Nestryn to Imrythel, then to my friend Jessa.

Though I had not announced a first advisor of my own, all assumed that I'd chosen my dearest friend. I had not, as I refused to accept that my father and our emperor wouldn't return. Jessa accepted her dismissal, but the others looked to my sisters, awaiting permission. Imrythel was the last to leave and made a show of pulling closed the heavy double doors.

Once alone with our holy counsel, the senior Hallowgale, Edamyn, began with the traditional opening blessing of the Triad. "May Atun, the All-Seer, guide us today."

Arlyn and Tasmynne dipped their heads acknowledging the tradition.

Arlyn offered the second invocation. "May Otarr, the Day-Seer, alight our way."

"And may the Night-Seer, Selene, give us wisdom," Tasmynne finished.

"Arlyn, do you wish to begin?" Edamyn held a shaky hand in the direction of Otarr's high priest.

"Yes, thank you." He sat straighter in his chair, folding his hands atop the table. "Otarr has shown Kōgō Noralynne Evangale the way to her next life. Time has passed enough that we may sweep the mandala sands. Emissaries from the Fire Forgers have delivered the phials. We have sorcerers at the ready to hold off any storms so we may ensure Otarr may gaze upon us. We are ready for the eighth and ninth rites to begin three days hence."

I stifled the urge to groan at the thought of two long, sweltering days under the sun overseeing the sweeping of the sands, and there would be no reprieve on the third as we handed out the phials of the ritual sands to the people. My sisters and I listened with aplomb as was our duty. Discussion continued between the Hallowgales around positioning and other technical aspects required for the ceremony, and I exchanged looks with my sisters from time to time until the insignificant details had run their course.

Tasmynne moved on. "As to the final rite, the caretakers are tending to the nymphs around the clock, keeping their ecosystem within the precise condition required to encourage the final transformation. The nymphs are preparing for their final molting cycle and are on schedule to emerge from the water and shed their skin just in time for the Rite of Release." Tasmynne relaxed back in her chair as she finished, clearly satisfied with the status of her preparations for the Nantai Rituals of Mourning.

In the swift pause that followed, Karynne leaned forward, resting her elbows on the table. "Very well," she said. "It seems all is on track to complete honoring our mother."

Just as swiftly, she turned to me and pinned me with a sharp gaze. Instinctively, I tensed, feeling my fingers digging into the wooden arm of the chair. As I scanned the others in the room, every person's focus also rested on me.

She continued, "Mairynne, are you prepared to tend to your duties once the rites are complete?"

I swallowed though my mouth felt suddenly dry. I'd foreseen this question, but that didn't make answering easier. Ultimately, I wasn't intent on abdication, only avoidance. "If you inquire about my understanding, I'm versed in the expectation that we begin preparation for my ascension."

"Expectation be damned to the hells," said Karynne. "What I wonder is if you actually plan to begin the proceedings. It is clearly what Father wanted; him having written his directive into the Stormskeep annals that you, his third daughter, shall be his successor to the throne of Stormskeep."

My shoulders tightened, my neck pinched, so I rolled my head to relieve the strain and sighed. While I adored my eldest sister, she could temper her rash demeanor with a smattering of tact. Leveling my voice as much as possible, I replied, "We have twelve sacred days remaining before I must face this decision, Kahry. Can we tend to our grief for now?"

Yasmynne reached across the table to offer me a hand. I accepted and awaited her thoughts. Her gaze flitted to our older sister, then with a gentle smile, she said, "Of course we will respect the rituals, but you should know that our people are becoming lost without a leader. Our advisors say there have been some disturbances in the streets, and we've heard rumors from the other castes."

The matter of unrest within the people concerned me more than my place on the throne; however, I needed time. "Twelve days," I responded, rigid and unmoving as I stated my will, "only then will I address the topic of inheritance."

"You must at least name your first advisor officially and make the decree in the annals," Karynne continued, seemingly searching for a way to force me to address my impending duty. "Jessa, though she is dear to you, is not an appropriate royal advisor."

Facing her, I pressed my lips into a tight line. There was little clarity in my mind as to why she believed Imrythel or Nestryn met the so-called requirements, but now wasn't the time to discuss. Pressing that issue would have only ensnared me in further conversation about a topic I wasn't ready to address. I turned to the elderly priest at my right and asked, "Is there aught to discuss regarding the rites?"

Edamyn Hallowgale replied, "No, Lady Mairynne, we have concluded our business."

I stood; the chair scraped against the floor as my momentum pushed it backward. My sisters both followed my cue. I hugged Karynne formally, then Yasmynne, who grabbed onto me and squeezed tight, showing the affection she wore in her very bones. As I broke the hug, I stated again, "Twelve days. It's not long. I value our sisterhood beyond what you will ever know, but this acceptance is mine and mine alone. I must come to it in my own time. Once I have decided, you both will be the first to know." On those words, I made for the doors.

Hot moisture gathered about my belts as I pulled one door inward enough to squeeze through and make my escape. In the foyer, I turned toward the open-air sanctuary overlooking Stormskeep Falls, desperate for some relief. In my path, Imrythel stood. My level gaze rested at the hollow in her long, graceful throat. Clenching my teeth, I lifted my chin to make eye contact.

◇◇◇◇◇◇◇◇◇◇◇◇◇◇◇

IMRYTHEL RAISED A HAND and softly ran a long finger down my face, the trail she traced burning a line from near my eye, down, and along my jawline. Against the urge to flinch away, I held myself in place and waited.

"Your sister cares deeply for you, for the Evangale

legacy, and for the Nantai people," she said, her voice deeper and more seductive than a woman's voice had a right to be. "I see many questions written on your face."

Unclear as to what she suggested, I reminded myself that Tennō Atheryn's decree named me successor and trained my features into a mask of solemnity. Versed in the ways of Nantai politics, the woman before me carried a manner about her that embodied power and temptation. She used her height to exude an air of authority while her curves dripped with sensuality, and the veil she wore covering one eye cast an air of mystery about her. In choosing her first advisor, my sister Karynne clearly sought to use these skills to her advantage. As Father had instructed us all, I measured my words. "Thank you, Imrythel. In these days, I take comfort in my sisters as we, along with the rest of the Nantai people, pay due respect to my mother's memory."

"Yes." She clasped her hands behind her back, and her gaze dropped for only a moment before she continued, "Well, do remember that you must have trust in those who love you."

I donned an appeasing smile and gave credit to the truth in her words. "Well put. Now, if you'll excuse me, I'd like some time in sanctuary with my thoughts."

As I moved around her, Jessa stepped to my side.

"Lady Mairynne," Imrythel called.

I turned to see that Karynne had joined her.

Regally, they stood shoulder-to-shoulder as Imrythel added, "Karynne and I both are to champion your path to the throne; your advocates if you will." She tipped her head forward in a move so small it almost escaped me.

Yet now was no time to bend in my conviction. Giving a single nod, I passed through the grand archway leaving them to their will and my dear friend in my wake. Inside, I clasped both of Jessa's hands and asked her to wait without, as well. I wished nothing more than to be alone with my thoughts and prayers to Atun and his children, Otarr and Selene. Deeper within the citadel, each of the Holy Triad had a dedicated chapel, but I favored this sanctuary, a sheltered balcony with three altars overlooking the Sundai Falls.

For time I didn't count, I knelt at Selene's altar and called a wind to bring mist from the falls and cool me as I contemplated. At intervals, I spoke aloud to the Gods, seeking guidance. I received no answers to the questions in my mind. Atun didn't tell me why someone slayed my mother; Otarr wouldn't grant me the knowledge of where my father had gone; and Selene gave me no guidance regarding my unsettling feeling that Tennō Atheryn still lived. Fighting a burning behind my eyes, I lifted my face to the skies and cried, "Father, what would you do in my place?"

An unseen, but rich and familiar voice answered, "I know not what Tennō Atheryn would do."

"Thalaj," I breathed, wiping a tear that'd strayed down my cheek. I stood and moved in his direction.

Arashi's first guard, *Gensui* Thalaj Northerngale, stepped from the shadows, from one of the apses set into the outer wall. Exempt from wearing full robes of mourning, Stormskeep guards dressed in light leathers with a red sash from shoulder to hip, easily removed should the need arise. Weapons remained accessible.

"Your robes flatter, but I do prefer your hair unbound," Thalaj said as he approached.

"These robes are better suited to my sisters than they are to me." I moved in his direction, but before I reached him, he dropped his eyes and turned slightly away. The movement prevented the embrace I'd intended, and my shoulders felt heavy again, this time not from the robes. "Will you not give me the comfort of holding me?"

"Lady Mairynne, you know it's blasphemous." He ran a hand over his braids to the thong at the base of his skull.

Flinching at the formality, I snapped, "We have done nothing blasphemous."

"If anyone sees us in an embrace, my head would decorate the spikes at the Stormskeep gates."

"No one can persecute you for offering comfort in this time." I searched his face.

He warned me off with a look and said, "That my mother is a Storm Sorcerer is insignificant here. That she chose a Frost Fighter as my father makes me unworthy. There is the matter of contamination that is punishable only by death."

"Thalaj," I huffed. "You know that I do not hold with the caste beliefs. And you know that my mother and father supported my stance."

"And how has that worked for them?" He challenged while rubbing a gloved thumb over the hilt of his scimityne. Seconds later, he realized the splinter his words had pushed under my skin. "I'm sorry." He dropped his head and silently moved to the railing beyond the altars, leaning over toward the falls.

I joined him. As he turned to face me, I could feel his eyes, and unable to handle the silence, I pressed, "Why must such things come between people drawn to one another?" My words were more of a complaint than a question.

He answered anyway, "Mairynne, you know how to change this."

I turned to him abruptly and questioned, "Not you too?" Everyone pressed for my ascension, but I'd hoped the man who'd become a fixture in my life, as our protector, wouldn't join causes with the masses.

Thalaj looked down. "It is not my place to counsel you, but royal decrees are our only mechanism for change amidst our people. An emperor or empress must formally write them into the annals under the Hallowgales' supervision. I see little other course of action."

Though his motivations were different, he'd joined in the opinion of the majority and clearly wished for my ascension. As such, I considered the personal conversation over, nodded, and switched to business. "Have you any word of my father from your network?"

"I do not."

"And you believe he will not return?"

"That, I cannot say for certain. Though there has never been a period when Tennō Atheryn has been absent from his castle for so many unexcused days."

I reached out over the railing toward the rushing water, calling for the mist. I concentrated, allowing the power to pool in my heart, and pulled with my sorcery. A small storm gathered in my hands. Watching the mist turn into tiny thunderheads and feeling rain begin to fall onto my palms, I absently asked, "Then why do I have this overwhelming sensation that he lives?"

Thalaj sighed. "I don't know, Lady Mairynne."

Silence except for rushing water and tiny sounds of

thunder cocooned us on the balcony. Calling on my magic offered a much-needed distraction and allowed an idea to bloom in the back of my mind. Stormskeep annals. The histories of our people written by rulers through the ages would surely offer guidance. I clapped my hands together, extinguishing the storm, and said, "I think . . ."

"What?" He searched my face. "What do you think?"

I glanced at him with a quirked brow and grin. "You, and everyone else, will see." Turning to the arched entry, I called the wind for assistance with my burdening robes and walked lightly and swiftly toward the foyer. Behind me, Thalaj's heels clicked upon the marble as he followed.

My sisters, their advisors, and the clergy still loitered in the foyer, likely awaiting my return. Jessa rushed toward me when I emerged; Karynne, Imrythel, and the clergy turned, but Yasmynne and Nestryn continued in their whispered conversation. I lowered my eyes, feeling a stab of jealousy over their happiness, but I refocused quickly. "Jessa," I said. "Send word to each member of Tennō Atheryn's advisory council that we will meet first thing on the morrow within the royal court."

"Of course, Lady Mairynne." Jessa curtsied, then scurried to the bridge and onward to complete the chore I'd demanded.

Yasmynne turned, alerted by my command. Karynne took a breath to speak.

Before she could utter words, I held up both hands to forestall her and said, "My sisters, Hallowgales of the Triad, and Imrythel and Nestryn as first advisors, you will all be in attendance as well at the ninth bell."

Karynne asked, "What is the meaning of the meeting?"

"You will learn with the others. Yasmynne, can you ensure that Aunt Nadialynne receives word and is present as well?"

She nodded, seeming uncertain and startled by the sudden demands which worked well to my taste.

My intent could remain a mystery for the time being. I turned to Thalaj before anyone else could utter more questions. I thought to ask for his company, but reconsidered and demanded, "You will escort me to the royal library."

TWO

A Scream in the Night

THE FORTY-NINTH DAY OF mourning arrived with little pomp, but I didn't have grief on my mind as I took a seat in the throne room of Stormskeep. I'd spent the remainder of the day before reading the histories and searching for an obscure solution to my dilemma. Yet, fortune hadn't favored my efforts. Almost an hour before the council would arrive, I sat on a chair I'd had placed in front of the throne, not wishing to make claim by sitting on the actual Serpentine Throne. The birds sang outside the open windows in the stone walls, and Otarr watched over Stormskeep from clear blue skies. Since I would present myself as leader at the meeting with the Storm Sorcery Council, I'd allowed Mother Feathergale to bind my hair as propriety dictated. At the end of the day, I would pay with pain throughout my temples and neck.

Still, tradition reigned.

Eerie silence turned into a clamor when the meeting's attendees and the guard arrived promptly at the ninth bell. My family and their first advisors procured seats to the left of the throne, the area designated for the ruler's family, the four leaders of each large Storm Sorcerer family to the right, and the clergy at the end of the long meeting table facing the throne. As the portly Havengale patriarch moved to his chair, I discerned a cut of his gaze toward my sisters and aunt, Nadialynne in particular. Then his eyes moved to the other three advisors in flitting glances. Did he hope I wouldn't notice his manner—that he seemed insecure amid the others on this council? I cleared my throat and he gathered himself, a smile plumping his cheeks further.

Along with the Storm Sorcery Council, Thalaj brought a retinue of city guardspeople and posted them outside the throne room. He stepped to my side and asked, "Is all well, Lady Evangale?" When I nodded tightly, he brushed a hand over mine and joined his team.

I held a hand out to a waiting Edamyn Hallowgale, signaling him to call the meeting to order.

He took a few timorous steps and struck the gong with a strength his posture belied. The commotion settled, and he invoked Atun's grace. In sequence the other priests called upon Otarr and Selene. When the Invocations were done, Tasmynne bowed and took her seat. Everyone turned toward me.

I pushed myself up from my chair and held both hands wide. "My fellow Nantai leaders, I've asked you here today to make a proposal."

A rumble went up, large for a crowd of only thirteen.

I closed my eyes briefly, awaiting silence. When the

questions faded, I said, "It is not my intention to declare for the Serpentine Throne at this time."

Another rumpus ensued to which I raised my hands further. Upon silence, I continued, "I do wish to hear your thoughts on this declaration. My sisters, Imrythel, Nestryn, and the Triad provided their thoughts in a private meeting yesterday at the citadel. But let us proceed in an orderly manner."

As such, my sisters sat quietly with mouths in tight lines. Nestryn reached for a goblet, and Imrythel remained hauntingly motionless, her sharp green gaze locked with mine. A chill ran up my spine, and I suppressed a shudder. To my right, I addressed the first of the Storm families, "Azurynne, please share the Nightingale concerns with the council."

The matriarch of the Nightingale family shifted in her seat. "Lady Mairynne, I mean no disrespect, but our people rely on leadership. Without an emperor or empress, thieves and murderers run rampant. From the days of Tennō Makenyn, the Storm Sorcerers have agreed that the leader keeps the laws and histories within the Stormskeep annals. Also, without a leader, there is no room for change. This is the first written law of the Nantai people."

Tipping my head to show respect, I said, "Thank you, Lady Azurynne. I do not intend to disregard the laws of Nantai, and what my forebearers have written weighs heavily on my decision. Is there aught you would add in the way of concerns from your family?"

"There is not."

I moved on. "Very well. Lukos? Will you share the concerns of the Thundergale family?"

The Thundergale patriarch stood and paced behind

the families, stroking the overlong hairs extending in a point from his chin. "My Lady of Evangale, on behalf of my family, I thank you for the opportunity to address you and this council in this manner. Although it is outside of protocol during the mourning rituals."

"Yes, Lukos. I am well aware of that, but given the circumstances, I felt certain this meeting was necessary."

Lukos continued, "That is a wisdom beyond your years, Lady Mairynne."

I held up a hand and addressed the entire council, "For the remainder of this meeting, we may dispense with the titles. I am seeking debate, if you will. I do not wish to get lost in the words that often make our proceedings lengthy. We must return to the sanctity of mourning as soon as possible." I scanned the room searching for approval. Nods affirmed, and to Lukos I said, "Please, continue."

"In the markets, our family has witnessed a series of uncharacteristic thefts since Tennō Atheryn disappeared. With the help of the guards, we have arrested several pickpockets in the streets. The holding cells in the city gates are nearing full. I know we only have a few days remaining, but I urge you to accept your duty as soon as our laws allow." He returned to his seat.

Addressing the third of the four families, I looked to Ohmyn. "And the council from Havengale?"

Ohmyn, rounder than most with thinning hair, blushed a bright red as he answered, "Our concern lies with the other castes. In the haven, we have heard rumors that many of the gnobles from the lower castes are developing plans to challenge the Storm Sorcerers for the throne. The rumors say that they believe having the empress murdered and the emperor disappear shows weakness within the Evangales, as well as across the Storm Sorcerer caste."

Disturbances in the marketplace along with the concern of not fulfilling the first law were of minimal concern compared to the lower castes contriving plans against the Storm Sorcerers. "Have you followed up with the guard on these rumors, Ohmyn?"

He shook his head vigorously enough that his cheeks billowed.

"Disregard the fact that it is business and do speak with Gensui Thalaj on the matter today or tomorrow."

"Yes, Lady Mairynne. I will bring my sons who heard the gossip to the guardhouse later today." At this, he fell silent.

I raised my chin to Solarynne Dawnsgale, the final of the four family leaders sitting on my father's council. Her look struck me, as it always did, with hair the color of an apple's inner flesh and eyes so light they almost seemed clear. Such light features were uncommon among the Nantai people . . . and truly haunting.

Accepting my cue, she said, "The Dawnsgale kindred have no qualms awaiting your decision, Lady Mairynne. Patience was one of Tennō Atheryn's best qualities and may be the very ingredient that ensures the peace we've known under his reign."

"Thank you, Solarynne. Aunt Nadia," I said, addressing her in the familiar, "my mother was your twin. Do you have counsel you wish to impart?"

Ohmyn Havengale interrupted, "Lady Mairynne? If I may?"

I raised a brow toward him, shocked by his insolence.

He blushed a deeper red, but adhering to my earlier

advice for candidness, he continued, "Your aunt has no place on this council."

"Master Havengale, I have called this meeting. You will see that my sisters sit here as well, and they are also not a part of this council. In the absence of my father's or my mother's wisdom, I wish to and will consult with my aunt." I turned back to Nadia, motioning for her to take the floor. "Please . . ."

"Mairynne," she started.

A stab of guilt pierced my gut as she spoke. I reached for the warm and cold tokens that hung about my neck. I'd distanced myself from my aunt after my mother's death, finding it difficult to look upon someone who was, yet who was not, the vision of Noralynne Evangale. Even her voice sounded similar in the lilt of her words.

"Nora," Nadia choked on her sister's name, swallowed, and continued, "my sister loved her children with her entire soul. But she was also a patriot of Nantai. She believed the gnobles should work together to unite the people and invite the Small Folk and the casteless into the politics of the country."

This caused an uproar from the council members. I held up my hand and waited until it had died down, then motioned to my aunt.

Nadia continued, "She gave her daughters room to grow into who they chose to be, and I believe she would stand by your instincts. I will honor what I believe would be her decision to support you in yours."

A lump grew solid in my throat, and I had no more answers than I had before. I couldn't find the words to speak for a long moment. My sisters, the Triad, and the rest present began to debate whether I should ascend to the Serpentine Throne or not, as if I were not present.

Quite possibly, I wasn't. My vision blurred as I considered. When I came back to myself, I cleared my throat as loudly as I could. Some of the conversation abated, but the last I heard, predictably, was Ohmyn's gravelly voice.

"There's also a rumor that the Ryū will awaken."

"Enough!" I shouted and stood. "My mother's grave is not cold. We have no evidence that the dragons are returning. We have naught to worry about from the castes. They hold the Nantai mourning period as sacred as we do. The Small Folk have never been of concern, and my mother lost her life in her desire to unite the lands.

"I spent the afternoon and into the evening yesterday reading the histories, looking for one case that might resemble our own. It saddens me to say I've been unsuccessful so far. I had hoped to have better guidance when I asked you here to propose that we wait until we have more information on Father's disappearance. Alas, that is what I propose, that we wait and that we send a team in search of Tennō Atheryn." With less gusto, I added, "But that does not seem to be on the minds of any of our people."

Nadia offered me a smile, but the others present sat in silence until Azurynne spoke softly, "Mairynne, such a decision is unprecedented, and we have no ruler to record the decree."

Nodding once, I prompted, "Then let us take a vote. Those in favor of executing the ascension as soon as the mourning is complete?"

Karynne, Imrythel, Azurynne, Lukos, and Ohmyn raised hands without hesitation. Yasmynne and the Triad followed suit, and Nestryn, of course, mimicked Yasmynne. I felt hollow. Did they not believe there was a chance for Father? And why were they all so certain that

I could handle the mantle of ruler when I, myself, held no such belief? In truth, beyond longing for my father's return, I wanted to see the world beyond Stormskeep and meet more of the people I'd rule one day. I'd been so sequestered here, in this castle, mostly apart from even the city below. Protected, my parents and caregivers had named it, but it felt like little more than a prison. I'd had so little experience with other castes. What were the Frost Fighters or Stone Singers like? I'd never met an Underhill Dweller, and I couldn't even recall the natures of the Cloud Courtiers. The casteless, the guilds within Nantai, the list went on and on. I had little but inexperience, ignorance, and naïvety to offer our people from where I'd lived within my stonewalled tower.

With a deep breath and losing hope with every second, I called for the alternative, "Those in favor of sending a search party for Tennō Atheryn?"

I raised my hand. Nadia and Solarynne did the same. The Triad and Lukos raised their hands as well for a second time in as many options. I felt my brows heavy as I turned to each of the latter one-by-one, questioning their meaning.

Lukos said, "Lady Mairynne, your question was flawed. If you mean to ask if I believe we should wait, I must lower my hand."

"That is what I intended, Lukos."

The Triad lowered their hands along with Lukos.

Defeated, I rolled my shoulders back. Eleven days remained, and I planned to spend that time with the history books searching for another solution. In the meantime, I made a choice. "Yasmynne, you will be in charge of the preparation for ascension. Do it quietly."

The most unlikely, carefree person in the room, she

gasped with widening eyes when I charged her with a task so important to the Nantai people. Others exchanged surprised glances.

Good. I'd turned the tables at least a little. "As for the rest, you will now visit the citadel and swear oaths that this decision will not go beyond these walls. I still have time to change my mind. You are dismissed."

◇◇◇◇◇◇◇◇◇◇◇◇◇◇◇◇

REACHING FOR MY STORM sorcery worked best with my eyes closed for reasons I'd never understood. In need of the wind, I did this now and reached out with my senses, pulling the air close and envisioning the path to my quarters. The thirteen sorcerers in council, as well as all the guards posted outside, also possessed storm magic— maybe theirs functioned differently than my own—but nevertheless, the sudden gust indoors would be of little consequence. As the wind gathered, I opened my eyes and rode the gale out of the throne room and all the way to my private door where I stopped and looked up and down the corridors.

Alone. Wondrously alone.

I barred the door and planned to remain alone for the long remainder of the day. It took me the better part of an hour to disrobe and release my braids; but once they were loose, I slipped into a gloriously soft tunic and a pair of pants. My hair, crimped and wild, rejoiced with the freedom. I refused knocks at my door, even with the promise of food. My stomach roared, but I ignored its demands. If they chose, my people could reach me by window, breaking another decorum.

My space held me in safety.

Under Otarr's bright watch and for the first time in forty-nine long days, my body rested easy, even if my mind did not. Throughout the day, I tried to distract myself with the epic songs recorded by the scroll workers, but my thoughts often strayed back to the notion I'd accepted my duty to become empress. Inside, I railed against it still. When frustration and anger overtook me, I hurled a scroll across the room and cried out, "Why, Father, have you left me to accept this responsibility? Why did you not name Karynne or Yasmynne? I barely have my majority!" I sank to my knees in the center of my room, arms raised to anyone or any being who might listen. "Do I not get a chance to live first? To learn of this world?"

I received no reply.

Twilight came, but before Selene took her position in the night sky, I donned a cloak, pulled a large painting away from the wall, and slipped through the hidden door within my rooms into a network of tunnels and stairs known only to royalty and a handful of those sworn to protect the secret. I carried two candles, one lit and the other in my pocket for the return to my chambers. Eager to be outside and no longer confined, I allowed my eyes time to adjust, then padded through tight spaces, around sharp curves, and down many winding stone steps until I found the exit a small distance from where the Sundai Falls crashed into the pool below. Built high enough into the stone cliff that others wouldn't know to look, the landing consisted of little more than a foothold. I extinguished and stowed the candle and called for the wind to lower myself the final distance onto the soft ground behind a copse of trees.

Beyond the trees, a public park lined the pool at the base of Stormskeep Falls. Mourning periods left public places empty, especially in the dark hours, so I ran freely between the trees and toward the soft grasses lining the poolside, my cloak billowing in the deepening night. Before reaching the water, I fell to my knees, breathed in the night's air, and allowed Selene to look upon my face, my hood falling away. I'd fought the urge to cry all day—anxious, angry, and wanting tears. Now, I closed my eyes, gathered moisture from the falls above my head, and let it rain down upon me.

Dampening minutes later, a rich voice called my name.

"Mairynne," it whispered, a warning wrapped up in the hiss of my name.

I smiled through my tears. "Thalaj. Come. Sit with me."

"Can you release your rain shower first?"

I did, though the damp grass remained. He knelt beside me, catlike in his posture and ready to pounce at the first sign of danger.

"How did you know to find me here?" I asked.

"That information is mine alone," he answered, his voice low.

I hadn't expected more. Thalaj kept his ways close to his heart, and he had a proven ability to find his way into spaces that seemed impossible. He'd come into our lives when I'd aged enough to have a budding affection for boys. Turn after turn, he'd shown his loyalty to the Evangales in many ways I knew, and I'm certain in ways only known to my father, Tennō Atheryn. Inside of Stormskeep, we had lived peaceful lives. With three quarters of the perimeter sheltered by the mountain, the city lay within stone walls and a wide moat provided a barrier to the outside. Visits to the domains of other castes were often tenuous, and Thalaj stood at my father's side everywhere he traveled. In a time before, my sister Yasmynne had gossiped of his work to thwart a would-be

Fire Forger assassin while the council of gnobles met at the High Cloud Court.

"Well enough," I said. "Did Ohmyn Havengale and his sons come to you today to discuss the rumors of caste uprising?"

"He did."

"And?"

"I have a team assigned. It's no matter for you to worry over during mourning."

"But I am to be empress before the moon goddess has completed her cycle," I spat, turning to look at him. "All of these matters are mine to worry over."

Thalaj gave me a tight smile but didn't speak. He didn't have to say a word to make his point.

After several silent moments, I relented. "You're right. You've proven yourself and your guard is more than competent to care for these matters, but we will speak of this once the mourning period has passed."

"Of course," he said.

We remained there on our knees and watching the water for some time until he said, "From the balcony, I heard your speech at the meeting this morning. Despite how afraid you must be, I believe it is the right decision."

I stared at him as heartbeats passed, trying to read beyond his stoicism. "It is what you wished. Is it not?" My words tasted sour as they passed my tongue and lips.

"It is, but not for the reasons you may believe." He bowed his head, grasping idly at the blades of grass.

"Then what are your reasons, Thalaj?" I searched his dark eyes, whether accusing or begging for answers, I couldn't be sure.

Instead of answering, Thalaj reached for me and I moved into him, resting my head on his shoulder. Being close to him never offered physical warmth, yet my very soul seemed to sigh. What his lean arms did offer were both strength and the closeness I craved, and I deplored that our culture forbade a relationship with this man solely because his blood contained two castes. If anything, shouldn't that make him superior to those of us with only one?

As we sat there in the silence of the night, a bone-shattering screech ripped across the sky, echoing from the stone castle, the citadel, and the rock faces surrounding the falls. The sound tore us apart.

Thalaj, somehow already on his feet, brandished his scimitynes, blue lightning crackling along the blades. My ears rang as I searched for the source. Water continued crashing into the pool, but despite the lingering vibration in my ears, there were no other sounds. The trees nearby remained motionless like the night.

"What evil could make such a sound?" I whispered to Thalaj.

"It's no sound I've ever heard," he replied. Sheathing his blades, he held a hand out to help me from the ground. "Maybe Selene is watching over you. Or bringing some warning. Let's go. I'll see you to your chambers." He pulled me toward the trees.

As Gensui, the head of our guard, Thalaj knew of the secret passages, so likely he knew that was how I had come to this place. I wondered briefly if he'd followed me but thought that an unlikely option since he hadn't been with me in my chambers. And he'd met with the family Havengale earlier.

When we came to the stone face, I brought the wind

to lift us both to the ledge. Thalaj went first, and I severed the flow of magic as I stepped behind the stone that hid the entrance. The blackness complete, I fumbled to find the candle. Thalaj clapped, and the friction of his palms scraped in the darkness. Soon, blue lightning danced in a sphere between his hands. With a smile, he shifted his energy to one hand and held it high. The glow cast an eerie, moving light on the stairs and set shadows to dancing upon the walls. But the orb lit our way back up into the castle, and eventually to my rooms.

Once there, I opened the door, pushed the painting forward, and stepped inside. Thalaj stood in the opening, telling me without words he'd not be entering my private space. How wrong it seemed that he'd offer the fleeting contact in the park yet he wouldn't cross the sacred line into my chambers . . . much like he wouldn't cross the lines drawn by caste. For this matter, I harbored bitter disappointment, yet I understood how to enact the necessary change. The cost was steep, but without the support of the Storm Sorcery Council, it seemed a price I must pay. Tightly, I nodded and leaned on the wall at the threshold.

"Goodnight, Mairynne. I'll find what caused that noise." He dipped his head respectfully, showing deference to my station.

"Listen, Thalaj. I understand that everyone believes my father won't return." I reached for the two stones at my neck. "Something tells me otherwise."

The fall of his face told me that even he believed otherwise. "I fear that you are overly hopeful."

"That may be true." I took his free hand. "But I would like you to send word through your network. If there is a possibility that he may resume reign over Nantai, I do not want to take the throne. He and my mother were wonderful for our people." I allowed my gaze to drop to our joined hands. "And I am afraid that I will not be." I felt more fear than I wished to acknowledge—heavy fear over being contained in this castle. Stormskeep held beauty and safety because by its very nature it was a fortress. But it also served as my stockade.

"Look at me, Mairynne."

I did.

"Tennō Atheryn was a wise man. He chose his successor with confidence, and you will do his memory justice." Thalaj had missed the breadth and depth of my worry.

My throat tightened. Clearing it, I said, "I appreciate the vote of confidence. But will you do as I ask?" I pleaded.

"I have doubts that I will learn aught we do not already know, but I will do as my future empress asks." He extinguished his sphere of lightning and lifted our hands. He brushed three kisses across my knuckles— more affection than he'd normally risk—then disappeared into the darkness.

THREE

The Mandala Sands

A LIBRARIAN DROPPED A STACK of books on the table, puffing a breath as she relieved herself of the burden. "Lady Mairynne, Lady Nadia, these are the annals from the Third Age, as you requested."

Looking up from my current read to see six new leather-bound tomes with the respective emperors' names scripted onto the spines further sucked at my optimism and determination to find a way out of taking over the Serpentine Throne. "Thank you," I said, not feeling in the least bit grateful. I sighed and slammed the current book closed, reaching for the next. "Kōgō Xenthyn has no solutions for me. Every decision she recorded seems to be in favor of increasing the ruling classes' power over the castes, the casteless, and the Small Folk. Why are our people so obsessed with all this hierarchy?" The notion disgusted me and degraded my mother's work to unite all

Nantai people.

My aunt offered no reply to my obviously rhetorical and plaintive question.

With arms folded, I leaned onto the tome and appraised my aunt across the table. I might endure for many moons and seasons before I could do justice to the task. Maybe such a notion, along with grief, clouded my thoughts. "Do you think I have lost my mind? Is all this worth the effort?"

She rolled up the scroll she was reading and set it aside. The look on her face said she was preparing to provide me with an appropriate and decorous answer. "What you are doing, my dear niece, is wise. Even if you do not find what you seek, all the history you'll have learned will be of great value to you as the Nantai empress."

The leather covering of the book felt smoothly worn under my thumb as I idly traced inlaid circular designs. "Nadia?"

She inclined her head and made a small *mmm* sound.

"Did you hear anything out of the ordinary? A terrorizing squall?"

"I did." She smiled and drew her brows to a peak. "Muffled, though, within my cottage. Likely one of the mountain birds of prey coming farther south than normal. I'm sure it's nothing to worry over."

I twisted my lips and chewed the inside of my cheek. It seemed an easy and logical answer, though I couldn't recall having heard that horrid of a noise from any bird. Although, I hadn't much worldly experience either, having been so sheltered inside Stormskeep at Arashi.

Perceptively, she asked, "There is more that troubles you?" And in her regard, I could see my mother. It'd been so hard to look upon my aunt, and wrongly, I still struggled with how much she reminded me of the one I'd lost.

"I owe you an apology."

"Whyever for?" She reached across the table, placing a hand on mine.

I couldn't look her in the eye as I answered, "I pushed you away upon my mother's death."

My aunt's soft laughter drew my confused attention.

She reached for a goblet and drank. "If you owe me an apology for that, I owe myself one as well. For the first ten days of mourning, I draped a sheet over every mirror in my cottage. Looking upon my own face felt like looking at Noralynne's, and I couldn't handle the sight."

"Would you tell me about her?" I asked. "Something new to me. I just want to feel close again for a few moments."

Nadia squirmed in her chair, but at last she said, "I'll tell you a story of both your mother and your father. Much of it also involves your oldest sister. It is one that holds many emotions . . . happiness, sadness, worry, loss. It embodies who Noralynne was as a person, how strongly she believed in the people, and how much she was willing to risk, yet it warns of dangers throughout our land." She looked around the library. "As we are the only ones here, I'll trust you with this, but your sisters, especially Karynne, mustn't know what I am about to share. I only know your mother's side of the story, but I'm certain Karynne has her own version."

I agreed, hungry for the information, another story. Grasping my goblet, I filled it from the pitcher and drank deeply while she gathered her thoughts.

She began, "At the time, Karynne was the only daughter of Tennō Atheryn and Kōgō Noralynne and a prized jewel of the Nantai people. To the people, she meant that the emperor had an heir and the Serpentine Throne would no longer be at risk. To my sister and her husband, she represented only their love. Karynne learned her words early and spoke in clear though simple sentences from the very beginning. She'd learned her letters and to gather the storm's magic long before other children her age, albeit only in small doses.

"As it turns out, you all did. You, dear Mairynne, may have been the slowest to learn these basics, but you were still ahead of your peers." Nadia offered a demure smile, then continued, "Tennō Atheryn and Kōgō Noralynne took ruling the people seriously. Your father held that the people—all people, big and small—were his reason for being. He rued when conflict arose between the castes and hated that the Frost Fighters and Fire Forgers were always positioning for rank within the people. Your mother, on the other hand, turned her attention to the Small Folk. Together, they believed that since Karynne would one day rule the Nantai, she should take part in their diplomatic interactions with the people."

I clung to every word about a life so different from what I knew at Stormskeep. Father had never permitted my sisters or me beyond the bordering walls, so to learn that this may not have always been the case both startled and thrilled me.

Nadia shifted, leaning back in her chair. "When Karynne was little more than seven, Noralynne took her along as she traveled to hold an audience with King Isao of the Small Folk at Brennmor. Upon their arrival, the armies of the emperor ambushed them at the gates. The guards took Karynne into custody on the orders of King Isao himself. Fearful of Noralynne's magic, he held

Karynne hostage under the threat of slitting her young throat at the first sign of storms on the horizon."

"Why would Isao do such a thing? Didn't he know my mother's intent?"

Nadia lifted a shoulder. Clearly Isao's reasoning never made it to her ears.

Dismayed, I mumbled, "And why would I have never known of this story?"

A touch ruefully, Nadia smiled. "The time that followed tested your mother and father's very beliefs on how to rule the people. It strained their relationship, and it took time to recover. Your father decreed that no one speak of the story. When you read his annals, you will see a line stating, 'The story of Noralynne, Karynne, and King Isao shall not be written and shall not be voiced, lest the teller spend the remainder of their days confined to the High Tower.' Until now, I have not shared what Noralynne confided in me. But, as you are about to ascend, I believe it is your right to know."

Taking a deep breath and trying to understand my father's motives, I motioned for her to continue.

Her eyes turned glassy as she went on, "Your mother spent more than ten days negotiating with King Isao. For the entire time, she used her storm magic to hold the clouds away from Brennmor. The Small King's ignorance as to the nature of our magic also kept him ignorant of the fact that she used her magic in this manner to protect her only daughter.

"In the end, Isao agreed to call off his guards and release the princess, and in exchange, Noralynne agreed to lessen the taxes imposed by Atheryn's father. Some considered this act by your mother treason, and in addition to Atheryn's anger, it put stress upon him from his advisors. The whole situation became the seed of disagreement between your mother and father. Although in time, Atheryn came to see she was right and wrote the decree, owning it as his own.

"That is their story though. The Small Folk guards returned Karynne to the empress in a sad state. To this day, we do not know what evil she experienced, but she'd lost enough weight that her eyes appeared sunken and bruised. Do you know of the rumors about the Small Folk?"

I tried to remember anything I'd read or heard, but I hadn't had a childhood like others where the younglings learned much of the comings and goings around Nantai through rumor on the streets. Father had sequestered me within Stormskeep. I had learned from the clergy, family, and tutors. Most play had been with my sisters. And my non-royal friends were chosen for me, much like Jessa or the occasional youngling of a caste gnoble, and we only associated under the supervision of a caretaker. With rumors being impolite in society, even younglings knew to avoid them when supervised.

I shook my head.

"I suppose not. Well, there are tales that the Small Folk who inhabit Brennmor and the city of Umbra within the Evernight Marshes feed on sorcery. If Karynne's brief time with them is any proof, mayhap the rumor is true. For the two seasons that followed, Karynne would speak to no one. I don't think she or your mother ever fully recovered. And after this, your father decreed that his children would not attend diplomatic missions until they had gained their majority and decided for themselves to attend." Nadia drained her glass.

After hearing the story, I felt heavier than I had before, but for different reasons. "My mother and father recovered from their disagreement, though? They always seemed to be so happily in love."

"Oh, yes." Her eyes lit up. "It must have been five or six years later, but they grew closer than they had been before. Within the next four years, Yasmynne and you were both born, bringing more joy to them and the realm."

"I heard my name," Yasmynne's sing-song voice broke into our conversation.

We both startled and looked up to my sister who stood beside the pile of annals.

"Delightful day, little sis. You're deep into the books, I see," she sang, wrinkling her nose. She leaned in to give our aunt a kiss on the cheek. "Aunt Nadia, how are you?"

After the pleasantries, she pulled a chair to my side. "I wanted to inform you of the plans for your ascension."

Speechless, I raised my brows, exchanging a look of sheer surprise with Nadia. This proactivity was especially unlike her.

Yasmynne continued, "I sent word to the Cloud Courtiers and received a prompt reply. The sky island will arrive the day after the last rites of mourning. Once the nymphs have gained their wings, we visit the sky island and attend the official High Cloud Court to discuss the plans."

My stomach clenched. Against my hopes that this would drag out under my sister's usual dalliance, it appeared we'd be moving rather quickly through the formalities. I'd never been to the High Cloud Court before, a place that wasn't really a place but castle grounds nestled upon a cloud in the sky. They traveled over Nantai constantly, given to the magic of the Cloud Courtiers who kept the floating grounds aloft. It enabled the castles to make lengthy journeys, retrieving gnobles from all corners of Nantai to convene in the High Cloud Court. I hadn't gained my majority the last time Father attended. Distantly, I asked, "What is it like in the Cloud Court?"

"Oh, Mairynne!" Yasmynne leaned forward, light twinkling in her eyes. "The regalia is so elegant it makes me tremble."

Naturally, the ceremonial attire and objects would be the first things to enter my sister's mind. She thought about things thinly, only reaching as far as the surface and relishing in things she could see. The tendency bothered me a little because she possessed the purest of souls beneath. I chuckled, knowing that I should be more specific when it came to such matters. "I'm wondering more about the proceedings."

"Well, remember how the meeting you requested two days ago progressed?"

Certainly it hadn't gone in the ways I'd hoped, but I answered simply, "I do."

"That is a mere sample of the ceremonial grandeur that transpires at the High Cloud Court. It should be an adventure. Nestryn and I plan to observe the proceedings of Comtesse Tsanseri's court whilst we are there." She put out her lower lip, then added, "Father wouldn't allow me into Love's Court the last time we visited the Cloud Courtiers."

Nadia and I exchanged another look. Clearly, my dear sister had ulterior motives for so aggressively pursuing the plans on my behalf.

At the far end of the library, the door flew open, commotion reverberating into the room and shattering the quiet. The librarian scurried from behind the desk and disappeared through the door. The noise intensified, furious footsteps shuffling through the stone corridor outside. I settled my gaze on Nadia, perplexed. She shook her head and pressed a hand onto the table, lifting herself from the chair. Yasmynne looked from me to my aunt in terrorized confusion too. I stood and hurried to the door.

OUTSIDE THE LIBRARY, GUARDS were rushing past by the dozens. I reached out and grasped one at the elbow and he turned to look at me, belatedly lowering his head when he realized my station.

"What is your name?" I asked.

"Perryn, my lady," he answered, waiting for me to release my grip.

"What is happening? Why has the city guard come to Stormskeep?" I demanded.

"Lady Evangale, there has been a body discovered. If you are safe in the library, I urge you to return to your activities."

Aghast that he'd insinuate I'd turn away from such a thing, I snapped, "Nonsense, Perryn. Where is this body?"

The librarian ducked her head and slunk back into the safety of the book- and scroll-lined room.

Perryn stammered.

I gripped his arm tighter. "It is clear that we don't have all day, Perryn." Furthermore, my heart raced at the possibilities. I thanked the Holy Triad that Yasmynne and Nadia were with me rather than somewhere else. But after Mother's and Father's fates, what of Karynne? Or my first guard, Thalaj? "I asked you where. I expect an answer."

"Your chambers, Lady Evangale," his voice choked on the words.

My stomach lurched. "Do you know who? Where is Gensui Thalaj Northerngale?" I couldn't stifle the latter question.

He shook his head and fidgeted with his leather cuffs. "They didn't say, but it is good to see you standing here alive and well."

"Well, let us not stand here any longer." I fell in with the soldiers moving toward my rooms. Thankfully, the corridor was open to the elements. I reached my hand out, closed my eyes briefly, and called for the wind. The gust at our backs moved everyone along faster.

I hadn't taken time to see if Yasmynne or Nadia followed, but when we reached my doors, Mother Feathergale stood outside, her shoulders shaking as she wept, a kerchief held to her mouth and covering her cries. I pulled her to me, wrapping my arms around her shoulders and shushing her as she clung to me and sobbed.

Guards rushed in and out, so many words flying I couldn't make sense of what was happening. When my attendant had finally quieted enough, I pulled back from her.

"Mother Feathergale," I asked, looking into her red-rimmed eyes. "What has happened?"

She wailed, "Jessamynne."

A jolt startled me straight, and I peered into the room where everyone huddled. Nadia arrived at my side.

To her, I asked, "Can you see to her?"

As soon as Nadia had nodded and taken Mother Feathergale in her arms, I pushed past the guards into the room, clearing my throat and standing as tall as possible. My chambers were sizable, but at the entry and toward the attendant area of the suite, the quarters were more cramped and certainly wouldn't hold dozens of armed guards.

I took a deep breath and from my gut bellowed, "Clear a path."

The guards molded themselves to the walls on either side, bowing their heads slightly as I held my chin high and passed by. At the end of the hall, I peered into the kitchen. I balled my hands into fists at my side to keep them still as I saw Jessa's twisted body on the floor, a tray of dishware and food splattered across the floor, and her once warm eyes staring coldly into space.

Thalaj stood on the far side, and as soon as he caught sight of me, the temperature in the room dropped sharply. He swore under his breath and circled the body in my direction. "Who let her through?"

When he reached me, I clung to him—all the while keeping my eyes on Jessa and trying to make sense of the scene before me—as he pulled at my shoulders, urging me from the room.

"Mairynne," he whispered in my ear. "I'm very sorry. We'll take care of this. You need not worry—"

I pulled away, swung back with my fist, and pounded it onto his chest. "How dare you believe I wouldn't worry about this? She was my oldest friend, and she's dead. In my rooms! And we have emptied Arashi's guards to come and see to the matter? Couldn't you have handled this more discreetly?"

He looked away then as two guards appeared at the end of my soldier-lined hallway carrying a litter.

Perryn was at their backs. "The healer, Sentei Summergale is preparing space, sir," he said to Thalaj.

My first guard nodded and waved the two with the litter through. "The rest of you, return to your posts." He pulled me to the side so the litter could pass. "We'll take her to the House of Healing. Mayhap Sentei Summergale can determine what has happened."

The guards left, a murmur rising as they made their way out of my chambers and away.

My eyes prickled then, a sense of small relief settling over me . . . confidence that Thalaj and the healer would get the situation under control and provide answers. "Who did this?" I whispered.

"There is no evidence that anyone is responsible."

I clung to him and he held me gently, both of us heedless of the watching guards. I assumed the impropriety seemed appropriate given the matter at hand.

Thalaj continued, "Jessa's mother states she left her alone in your rooms where she was preparing a midday meal for you. When the elder Feathergale returned, she found her daughter as you saw her now. She ran to the guards posted at the keep's entrance who sent word to me. I have only arrived in the last few moments myself. No one has moved her until now."

The extra guards cleared out, and one of the two who had brought the litter poked his head out from the kitchen. "My lady, may we use your blanket?"

"I'll get it," a strained voice called from the door. Mother Feathergale scurried into the room, wiping the tears from under her eyes.

I went to her and grasped her arms, turning her to me. "You just found your daughter. You should take some time." Nadia had followed her inside, and I waved her over. "Mother Feathergale, you do not have to tend to me in your own time of need. We will find another."

Her lip quivered. "No, Lady Mairynne. You and your sisters are as much daughters to me as my own Jess— Jessamynne." She covered her mouth with a fist and paused. A minute or more passed, but when recovered, she continued, "And I'd worry about you the entire time. I cannot promise I'll not weep from time to time, but please, allow me this. Caring for you and your rooms is all I know."

◇◇◇◇◇◇◇◇◇◇◇◇◇◇◇

MY FAMILY GATHERED AT the pyre fields. The day before, intricate mandalas of brightly colored sand had covered the ground, designs meant to offer my mother up to the Gods so they would guide her safely to her next life. In the natural course of death, the bodies of emperors, empresses, and clergy would be entombed so that while their corporeal presence remained on land, their souls were freed to pass into the heavens and find their eternal homes aside Atun, Otarr, and Selene. Since Kōgō Noralynne had been murdered, the teachings of Atun dictated that she should be offered another life via a grand fire. In the ceremony following the pyre, my mother's ashes had been blended with colorful sands which the acolytes of our Holy Triad shaped into intricate sacred mandalas across the scorched land. Yesterday, when my dear friend Jessa had left this life and we transported her body to the healer in hopes he'd discover the cause of her death, the acolytes had swept my mother's sands. On this day, we gathered for the Giving of the Sands.

Jessa would receive little of this ceremony, only a simple pyre to see her to the next life. I turned from the field, closing my eyes, fighting tears, and now believing she and my mother had been far more fortunate than Father. If he had indeed met his death and hadn't received the rites of mourning through entombment or pyre, he would never meet Atun. He wouldn't walk with Otarr and Selene into his next life, and his soul would never shine in the night's sky. If I accepted his disappearance without the offering of his body through funereal rites, his soul would forever wander the land—lost.

The tragedy of my father's fate twisted my belly, and though I felt within the deepest part of me he still lived, the solution to finding him eluded me.

Today, our people, my people, would come to receive the Holy Sands so they might take home a piece of their empress. My sisters, Nadia, and I would greet each person in turn and hand them a phial. Where they would keep these sands within their homes, I did not know, but our traditions dictated that every one of her subjects had a right to own a token of remembrance of their ruler, my mother.

Along the north side of the square field, I walked the length of the platform, past thousands of tiny glass phials corked and arranged in neat rows, to meet my sisters. Though Otarr had only risen a quarter of the way into the sky, a trickle of sweat rolled down my back.

Karynne opened her arms to me as I approached and I hugged her.

She whispered in my ear, "I heard of your loss. 'Tis difficult, I'm sure, to be here today. May Selene heal your heart, Sister."

"Thank you," I said simply, then hugged Yasmynne, then Nadia.

Imrythel and Nestryn were also on the podium as my sisters' first advisors. My aunt, not believing herself royalty, had not named a first advisor. Instead, her partner, Corwyn Dawnsgale, stood at her side, offering a warm smile.

Much to Karynne's dismay, I'd arrived alone.

"After today, you must choose an advisor, Mairynne," commanded Karynne, Imrythel at her side and Nestryn at Yasmynne's.

Standing straight and holding my ground, I replied, "Today, of all days, is not the day to worry over first advisors. I have also chosen to defer selection of advisors for my council for a time. Do you wish to judge me in that matter as well?" I caught a green light, a glint from Imrythel's hard stare, and locked gazes with her one unveiled eye.

Yasmynne furrowed her brows. "I thought you would have selected Jessa."

"Jessa was a loyal friend, indeed," I replied, my throat tightening as I held eye contact with Karynne's named advisor. I swallowed and asked, "Imrythel, is there aught you wish to say?"

She smiled, and though it seemed in deference, something told me otherwise. Her head slightly tilted, she said, "It is only that the Sandsgales have not been a part of the royal council in the past. We are anxious to serve the Serpentine Throne, Lady Mairynne."

"I see"—but her words felt contrived—"and would you suggest I select someone from your family from the Great Sands near Yōtei? A Storm Sorcerer whom I have never met, mayhap?"

The bells began to ring, snipping the conversation, and any reply she might offer, short. The acolytes of the citadel, servants to Atun, Otarr, and Selene alike, opened the gates into the pyre fields. Reluctantly, I turned my attention.

People, thousands of people dressed in mourning robes, waited in the streets beyond and began to filter inside from the east. They walked the perimeter along the south, then the west, many stopping at some point and calling a tiny gust of wind into a handful of rose petals. The winds showered the petals onto the clean-swept pyre field and represented the people's gifts and well wishes to the fallen in her next life. Others knelt and dropped packages at the edges of the field—an action marking them as either casteless or of a lesser caste who had no powers to call forth and shower petals over where my mother had burned. After their offerings, each Storm Sorcerer walked the northern side and received his or her phial from one of the family before returning to the eastern gates. Tradition restricted the casteless and lower castes from standing upon the family's podium, so they accepted a phial from one of the clergy members instead.

A pause in the steady stream of people came after some time, and Imrythel took the opportunity to further her case. "Your father, Tennō Atheryn, only selected from the families at Stormskeep. I'd beg you to consider those from outside the city's walls. If not as your first advisor, at least for one to sit on your private council."

I held my tongue, not wanting to mar the sanctity of one of our most sacred rituals.

Karynne supported her advisor. "Expanding your council to include more of the Nantai people would be Mother's wish, do you not agree?"

I glared at my sister but forced a smile as the next group of people approached. Retrieving a handful of phials from the table, I distributed them. An older man, stooped and limping, came forward and accepted the last phial in my hand. He then offered me his own hand to shake. When I accepted, his skin felt paper-thin, but the strength with which he gripped perpetuated the dichotomy. And his eyes held a youth at odds with his bent posture. They were dark gray, and within his right pupil there was a white fleck, a malformation of sorts. He smiled warmly, and I felt that the heavy robes and my sweating under Otarr's gaze were a price well paid. "May Atun watch over you, kind sir," I said, attempting to bring myself back to center.

His voice hale and an octave higher than I would have imagined and somewhat forced through the nose, he replied, "Many, many thanks, Lady Mairynne Evangale. May Otarr fill your days with joy, Selene guard your soul under her silvery light, and Atun care for your path to the Serpentine Throne."

As he went, I watched him limp away for long minutes until he had passed through the gates and out of sight. My brow felt heavy, and I chewed the inside of my lip as I puzzled over the person.

"Mairynne," Karynne recalled my attention.

I swung my head around and snapped, "What would you have of me, Sister? Things are simply too difficult to make rash decisions at the moment. Would you also advise that I include a Northerngale? An Islandgale from the Vesterisles? Any of our brethren from southern Nantai?"

The others in my family looked on surreptitiously as I debated with my eldest sister and Imrythel, but they continued to tend to their duties. Corwyn, having retreated into the citadel, returned with water to quench our thirsts and stave off the heat for another hour, and the acolytes held off the people while we partook.

Imrythel refused the offer, instead responding, "If that is the will of the future empress, we would find that an equal and appropriate measure." Her words stung as if she were trying to manipulate me through deference.

I answered, "Never before has an emperor or empress demanded one of our people leave their clan to sit in an advisory council. It is why we conduct the true business of the realm at the High Cloud Court in regular cycles. What makes us important enough to make demands that would separate families for longer periods?" I sighed and more quietly said, "I am uncertain why I would begin such a tradition."

"Sister," Karynne admonished. Her defense of her first advisor rang true and steady when she continued more quietly, "Imrythel only means to include the more nomadic families."

I raised my brows to her, offended that she'd stand by someone who didn't belong to our family on such a day, heavy in the heart that she wouldn't hold more compassion for all I'd just been through. My dismay came out as an accusation toward her too. "Ah, so would you also recommend that we include a representative from the Tsinti?"

I had grown weary of the conversation, and my words were shorter than necessary, intended to stop her suggestions. I knew this wasn't her implication. The Tsinti were nomads who lived apart from the people by choice. They were us, but not. They chose to eschew our traditions in favor of roaming the lands hidden under tsym.

As my ire continued to build, I pressed my rebuttal harder. "And what of a Cloud Courtier? A Frost Fighter or Fire Forger? Maybe a Stone Singer and an Underhill Dweller? And let us not forsake the Small Folk or the casteless." Heat kindled inside as I rattled off every group of our people that came to mind until Nadia placed a hand on my arm.

She rested the other on Karynne's. "This is a conversation for another time."

Lifting my chin, I spat, "It most certainly is. We should return to our people and the Giving of the Sands." Quieter, I added with chagrin, "Thank you, Aunt Nadia."

"Mairynne," Karynne started.

I whirled on her but felt intent on bringing the conversation to an end. "My dear sister, I have duly noted your requests, but our aunt speaks true. We are spoiling this rite for us and for our people. The Rite of Release will follow in a week's time. I have until the day after when I am to host an audience at the High Cloud Court to address such matters. Today, let us honor our traditions."

My speech worked as desired and silenced the topic. From then on, we went about the rite in companionable silence, holding light and idle conversation throughout. Mother Feathergale, her eyes still swollen from her abundance of tears shed, brought a late afternoon meal for the family and the Triad called a pause so we might dine.

Later, as the sun began to set, the last of the people trickled through. Edamyn approached when all had passed to let us know that they were shutting the gates and the acolytes would begin cleaning. Over the quieter course of the later hours, I'd thought more and more of the need to find my father. I turned to my eldest sister. "Karynne, have you given thought to the party we'll send in search of Father?"

Both she and Yasmynne gaped, eyes wide and jaws working but failing to produce words. I hadn't expected otherwise, but like they both had their own agendas, I had need to pursue my own. "Karynne, I've asked Yasmynne to plan for the ascension ceremonies. Whilst I am considering my advisory council and first advisor, I'd like you to take charge of this matter and put out a call for a party who will accept such a duty and search the lands for Tennō Atheryn."

Karynne closed her mouth and hesitated, then curtsied. I did believe I'd succeeded in shocking my eldest, most poised sister into submission, if only for a time. She bowed, then turned toward the citadel to make her exit.

It was progress.

Imrythel dipped her head and joined my sister.

I turned to Nadia, who said, "You've recovered well, my niece." She chuckled as she looked after them. Then she took my arm and pulled me in the direction of the castle; Corwyn walked at her side. As we went, she asked, "I may have missed him, but did Thalaj come through today?"

FOUR

A Family Meal

My ATTENTION SHOULD HAVE been on Stormskeep's annals. I should have been continuing my search for a way to avoid ascension as I still felt too young, too naïve, and too broken to assume the position. Yet my eyes had grown tired of reading scripts in the library's dim light. I needed to be outside, to feel the fresh air, and to be able to call a cyclone to life if I wished, and to work out my frustration over losing my childhood friend.

True, there existed no space in Stormskeep large enough for a storm as grand as I longed to call. I settled for the open sanctuary at the citadel where the balconies curved around and offered views of Sundai Falls, the castle itself, and an expansive park a level down the mountainside.

I paced.

Fondling the tokens I kept on a chain close to my heart—one cold and one hot, one from my mother and one from my father—I walked back and forth along the railing. Worry over what seemed would be my fate whether I wished it or not gnawed at me.

Tasmynne, servant of the goddess Selene, approached. "Lady Mairynne, the acolytes have brought a tray of fruit and cheese. Is there aught that I may do for you? Something to ease your broken heart, perhaps?" Her eyes held all the benevolence of the Gods but little in the way of solution.

With a sigh, I stopped and gathered her hands in my own. "I cannot think of anything you may do to change my course. You are not at liberty to leave this place and search for Father any more than I am. Though I appreciate the sentiment."

When she departed, I leaned onto the railing overlooking the open field below. Stormskeep's guards trained. Face after soldier's face paired off in combat, each wielding a unique weapon. When my gaze traveled to the far end, I spied the very person I longed to see.

Thalaj.

No other soldier in the Arashi guard moved in the same manner, a style he'd perfected during his time with the Unseen, using weapons others had always failed to master. I watched him work dual blades against his opponent. The short, curved scimitynes reflected Otarr's light as Thalaj executed twists, slashes, and blocks, the blades seemingly an extension of the person himself. But clearly, he went easier on his opponent than his skill would allow. He made a final parry with the curved blades crossed over his head, they parted and bowed to each other, then he sheathed his curved daggers. Mayhap he felt that I watched because he turned and lifted his face to where I stood. Across long space, we connected with our eyes alone until he gave a single nod, said a few words to his sparring mate, and strode off the field.

The other soldiers continued to spar, and I moved away from the railing and back several times in my course of pacing, each time scanning those sparring to see if he'd returned to the field. Mayhap an hour had passed when a cool breeze preceded his silent arrival at my side, a whisper that let me know he approached.

I could scarcely contain the urge to ask what his network may have learned, so by way of greeting, I asked, "What news?" as I hurried toward him, wondering of both Jessa and the errand I'd sent him upon regarding Father.

He stopped, lowering his eyes and answered, "Sentei Summergale cannot find cause for your servant's death. The attendants have taken Jessamynne Feathergale's body to the common pyre fields."

My heart dove at the news of my friend. "When do they plan the pyre?"

"Tomorrow."

I nodded. "I'll be there."

"Regarding the other matter, there is hope," he said.

As if lifted then by the wind, my soul soared. With news of hope, I felt lighter in my mourning robes than I had since Father's sudden disappearance. I laid a hand on my guard's arm and smiled. My next words tumbled forward, "Wonderful to hear. Whatever knowledge you have gained will aide in the plight. Will you share the news? I've asked Karynne to gather a party to begin the search."

Thalaj's expression turned to stone.

I searched his face. "You disagree with my choice to

arrange the search party?"

"You will be my empress. I am not at liberty to disagree," he answered, slipping from under my touch.

Scoffing at the propriety, I snapped, "That I will become empress—against all I desire—holds no power over your right to agree or disagree."

"That is not the common opinion, Mairynne." His temper and tone remained even, no hint of accusation entering his words, only fact.

I lost a bit of fuel as I said, "Well, it is mine."

Lips pressed tightly together, he gave a small, unconvincing nod. "I'll speak with your sister as you wish. I do have some thoughts on who might be a wise choice to go in search of Tennō Atheryn."

This course of conversation seemed sound enough as I sorely wanted to know what he'd learned from his shadowy spies. "Will you tell me the details?" As his ruler, I had the right to ask or even demand the information, yet I did so with caution, aware that he kept the secrets of the Unseen Guild close to his chest.

The ask didn't seem to offend, and he answered easily, "My sources said we should approach the Tsinti."

The mention of the notorious nomadic people, the Nantai wanderers of the grasslands, shocked me back into pacing. He watched with his classic stone-jawed stoicism as I processed all that this might mean. At length, I returned to him with arms folded across my chest. "What you say is impossible. No one finds the Tsinti. They are the ones who find the people they wish."

"Your concerns are well noted, Lady Mairynne. Even in my network, there are no known ways to find the Tsinti when they cast tsym over their caravans. Though the information still offers some slight hope." He clasped his hands behind his back, a soldier's restful position.

I clenched my teeth, released, and said, "That is not what I'd call hope." Any optimism faded fast as I looked away, my vision blurring behind angry tears. This wasn't how a leader should behave, certainly not the demeanor of an empress. I cursed the tears that presently revealed little more than my youth.

"Mairynne," Thalaj said softly and stepped close enough that I felt his cool presence again. "Come here." He wouldn't take me into his arms without my consent.

Understanding that the command reflected more invitation than demand, I went, heedless of propriety. And once in his arms, my tears flowed.

Soothingly, he said, "Crying over your father and after you lost a friend of many years does not make you weak, and yes, hope does remain."

I chuckled at that. Even though he was a guard and considered beneath my stature, he knew me better than most. I pulled away, swept my hands under my eyes, and asked, "How? How is it possible to find these hidden people?"

"There are rumors of a totem held by the Small Folk of Umbra within the Evernight Marshes. Rumor holds that this trinket has the power to allow its holder to see through a Tsinti tsym."

I gasped, recalling the story Nadia had shared of Karynne and the rumors of the Small Folk. "Do we have anyone who can navigate the marshes and withstand whatever dangers they pose? I worry about assigning someone unfamiliar with such a place to the search party."

A thought he clearly didn't wish to voice pulled his gaze from mine.

"Thalaj?" I asked, ducking to regain eye contact. "What are you considering?"

"I know of no other person who has entered and returned from the marshes, aside from me."

Pinching the bridge of my nose in suspicion of another dead end, I asked, "So, if there is no one, what do you suggest instead?"

He made no reply.

I inhaled sharply, my voice just as sharp as I pressed, "What are you suggesting, Thalaj?"

If he felt an urge to flinch away from my appalled question, I'd have never known. Instead, his words remained level. "I think you know the answer to that question."

"No," I commanded. "There must be another way. I cannot be without you to lead my guard." But there was so much more twisting around in my mind. *I cannot ask you to face this danger. And I cannot be without the hope for us*, I didn't say. Weaker then, I questioned, "I've lost so much already, and now you'd leave me too?"

A glimmer flashed in his dark, slanted eyes, but after examining my face, he reapplied his solemn mask. "I have already spoken with Tarlyn. He will assume leadership of the guard in my stead. I'd trust him with my life, and you can rest easy doing the same." He swallowed, then added, "It may also do us some good to be apart."

"For what reason would separation do us good?"

"Again, I believe you ask for answers you already know." Thalaj spoke truly, yet I disagreed.

Through gritted teeth, I said, "I want to hear you say it."

"My blood is impure, and for us to be together would contaminate you. The Nantai people are slow to change, and I fear they would not tolerate such a declaration, even from their empress. It flies in the face of the caste system. By blood, I am as much Frost Fighter of the fourth caste as I am Storm Sorcerer." He paused and sighed. "Mairynne, I feel us growing closer. I sense your desire to deepen that, but I"—he shook his head—"I just can't."

Ill within my very core, I spun from him and resumed the path I'd been pacing. To further my dismay, I did understand the reason in Thalaj's logic, or mayhap I suspected it ran deeper. And that he wouldn't share hurt even more. When I'd exhausted my immediate frustration, I sat on the kneeler at Selene's altar, face lifted toward the sky as if to ask why, and said, "Well and so," defeat resounding in the small customary acceptance.

It was as much as I could muster.

Thalaj came to me, near enough that I felt a chill but taking care not to touch. "I will update you after I speak with Lady Karynne." He turned both my hands upward and placed a kiss on each palm—a symbol of servitude to a ruler of the people. He then bowed to me and left.

I cried.

And afterward, while upon that kneeler, long hours passed in stillness—so many that night had transpired by the time I gathered my wits and stood. Anger constricted around my chest, more so than the heavy belting, and I'd come to a decision there at Selene's altar. And it was a plain one. I had to find a way to break free of all these barriers and make the things I desired happen.

I went to Nadia's cottage, still within the castle's

grounds but apart from the main keep and the wings where the royal family resided. Gifted to her by my mother who wanted her twin close, it stood inside a swath of greenery and flowers. When I knocked, Corwyn answered wearing his evening's attire and a mask of concern. I breezed past him without greeting and into the sitting room where my aunt lounged.

"Nadia," I said urgently. "Tomorrow. We must figure out a way to change the course of things. Time is running out, and I won't become empress. I cannot. I am not ready. The only option is to find my father and restore his reign, but we must find something in the annals that lawfully allows for this."

Nadia stood, a sheath dress flowing around her long limbs as she came to me. She and my late mother both stood a head taller than me. My sister Karynne had their height. Yasmynne favored the women of my father's blood, and I fell somewhere in between. I wished for height as it seemed to give Karynne a confidence that I longed to possess but did not.

"Dear Mairynne, we are looking as fast as we can. Why has it become so urgent this evening?" my aunt asked.

I hung my head. "Thalaj wants to lead the party we will send in search of Father. They must travel into the Evernight."

Nadia sighed and exchanged a knowing look with Corwyn. She placed an arm around my shoulders, guiding me gently in the direction of her long sofa. We sat.

"Maybe we should go tonight," I said, urgency coursing through my blood. "We still have four ages of royal decrees to read. How are we ever going to get through all that and find a lawful solution before I must go through ascension?"

Corwyn cleared his throat. "If I may, Lady Mairynne?" He waited until I nodded for him to continue, then said, "My cousin, Solarynne supports your plight. I believe she showed as much at your council meeting. She's aged and wise and may be able to offer some advice if you would allow me to beg her help."

Though I remained uncertain how she might be able to help, the thought was still an unexpected delight. "Of course, Corwyn," I said. "I can use all the willing help available."

Nadia grabbed and squeezed my hand. "We'll find an answer tomorrow; I feel it."

I turned to my aunt. "We must. I cannot shake the feeling that Father lives, and I intend to have him returned to Arashi and Stormskeep so he may resume his rightful position upon the Serpentine Throne." I stood. "And somehow, someway, I intend to accompany Thalaj on the journey to bring him back."

◇◇◇◇◇◇◇◇◇◇◇◇◇◇◇◇◇◇

I'D GROWN SLEEPY AT Nadia's cottage and stayed in her guest rooms for the night. The following morning, Corwyn left us at dawn, and my aunt's housemaid Larynne prepared plates of fruit and bread and served barley tea at its side. After Nadia and I had broken our fast, Solarynne Dawnsgale arrived on the patio at Corwyn's side on a gust of wind. Her hair settled over one shoulder, the cream-colored waves unexpectedly tame. She came to me with a grin and one hand forward. I accepted, my hand open to the sky, and she laid a kiss upon my palm.

As she raised her head and ice-clear eyes found mine, she said, "I began to believe you wouldn't ask for help, young one. Imagine my delight to receive my dear brother just as Otarr arrived this morning."

"Thank you for coming, Solarynne." I'd redressed that morning with the help of Larynne, my aunt's handmaiden.

"Corwyn," she continued, "was right to suggest you seek my help. I've studied our royal histories for many years, and your father's royal council was the third on which I've served." She looked beyond me.

Nadia circled from behind our breakfast table and gave Solarynne a hug and a kiss on the cheek.

Solarynne asked, "Have you finished your morning meal?"

Nadia answered, "We have. We were visiting whilst we awaited your arrival."

"Very well. Shall we go to the royal library and begin?" The suggestion erased a decade from her age.

As we left Nadia's small garden home and entered the halls of stone, Solarynne continued, "There was an empress in the Second Age, Kōgō Phelyse. The second ruler of that age, I believe. She may be our best option to find your solution, though she was quite prolific."

At the juncture of two halls, we turned right toward the library that lay deeper within the mountain, cooler, dryer, and darker than other areas of the castle; thus to better preserve the Nantai records. We passed two young attendants who moved to the side, showing deference to our royal station. I slowed and bade them each good morning, the action drawing confused and awestruck looks between the two.

With a curtsy, the girl replied, "Good day to you, Lady Mairynne."

The boy bowed. "And may the Triad watch over

you."

"And you as well." I smiled warmly to them both and continued on my path. It confounded me why people I'd spoken easily with not more than two moons before felt the sudden need for such extreme propriety. Yes, I expected the reaction. Yet it still rankled. The fact I was now heir apparent didn't change who I was in my heart.

From behind I heard, "Mairynne!"

I turned to find my sister Karynne and Imrythel moving with windswept speed toward the four of us.

"Where have you been? I went to your chambers both last night and this morning but found them empty." My sister wrapped me into her long arms. "We were worried."

Over her shoulder, Imrythel stood stoically, almost judging, watching. When released, I asked, "We?"

Karynne made a small sound but didn't answer directly.

Nadia stepped closer. "Good morning, Karynne. Mairynne, we'll get started inside." And with the few words, she, Corwyn, and Solarynne continued down the hallway and disappeared through the library's door at the end.

"Did you have reason to meet with me, Sister?" I asked.

Softly she said, "I bring some news you might find troubling. Gensui Northerngale has volunteered to lead Father's search party."

"I am aware. We spoke about it yesterday." I lifted my chin higher, working to keep my manner even-keeled.

"Ah, I see."

Clearly, my first guard hadn't been as transparent with my dear sister as he had with me about the reasonings and his intent. It gave me some solace, but not enough. "Have you gathered others? Or did he suggest others? And when do they propose to depart?"

I glanced again past my sister to the green-eyed beauty who accompanied her at seemingly all times lately. Something seemed different about Imrythel this morning, but I couldn't place it. Were the angles of her face a bit longer? Maybe she'd lost some weight. It would be understandable for one spending so much time with my sister.

Karynne answered, "The party won't leave before the conclusion of the mourning period.

I felt of different minds—relieved to have more time, devastated that a longer wait remained, and concerned whether Thalaj would find answers I needed in time. Trying to keep sincerity in my voice, I said, "Wonderful. And the others?"

"Imrythel and I will be working on finalizing those details today. May we share evening meal? I'll ask Yasmynne to join us."

Considering her request, I walked through the remainder of my day in my mind. After research here at the royal library, I needed to attend the common pyre grounds with Mother Feathergale. The last thing I wanted after that was to be in a position where I had to play politics.

I countered, "I'd like to dine with family tonight. Alone." I looked meaningfully to my sister's advisor, the black lace blocking half of any emotion she might betray through her piercing eyes. "Send word to Yasmynne, and I'll have Mother Feathergale and her new assistant prepare a table in my chambers."

An objection started within my sister's throat but died quickly. "Of course."

"I'll see you in the evening, Karynne." I turned and left my sister and her first advisor standing in the hall. Slowly, I expelled a breath along with the tension I'd held within my lungs.

Inside the library, the attendant greeted me in much the same manner as the young boy and girl in the hall and pointed me to the small room where Solarynne, Corwyn, and Nadia had already started in on a stack of annals from the Fifth Age.

Nodding into her book as she read, Solarynne looked up as I took my seat. "I believe we've found your answer."

<><><><><><><><><><><>

A COMMONER'S FUNERAL CARRIED far less ritual than one from the royal house. The family and close friends gathered and placed flowers around the body upon the pyre bed, then stood back. An acolyte of Atun dripped a drop of blessed water onto Jessa's lips. Selene's representative covered my friend's body with a white shroud to keep out the impure spirits, then Otarr's priest placed a knife upon her chest to drive away the evil as her soul lifted from the flame and went in search of her next life.

In the closing measure, the family and friends each lifted a torch from a nearby fire and placed it under the pyre bed. We moved away and watched in silence.

I wrapped an arm around Mother Feathergale's shoulders, and we cried silently. I prayed to the Holy Triad that Jessamynne's soul would be reborn among our people and find a happier end in her next life.

◇◇◇◇◇◇◇◇◇◇◇◇◇◇◇◇◇

PREPARATIONS FOR EVENING MEAL were well under way when Mother Feathergale and I returned to my chambers. Roasted fowl scented the air, and my mouth watered. I moved to my bed chamber and released the braids from my hair as my attendant took charge.

When I entered my main chamber, the new assistant to Mother Feathergale, a young Storm Sorcerer by the name of Dorynne, was putting the final touches on the table.

She curtsied when she caught me watching. "Lady Mairynne," she said, and her cheeks pinkened.

I smiled. "Continue with your business, Dorynne."

I wondered about the actual preparation of the food. In all my days, someone else had always prepared my meals, and it struck me now as a skill I might soon wish to have. Though I hadn't asked for the comforts royalty offered, it had been what I was born to as the daughter of the Nantai emperor and empress. I also wondered if my sisters had ever had occasion to roast a bird or bake a vegetable tart.

Mother Feathergale offered me warm glances as she worked but remained mostly silent while tending to her duty. We'd shared another sad day over her daughter and my friend, and my heart ached for her as much as it did in the absence of Jessa herself.

Mother Feathergale filled the goblets, and as she poured, I asked, "Is it difficult?"

She didn't look away from her task as she replied, "I'm sorry, dear. Is what difficult?"

"Making a meal. Cooking, I imagine."

Her brows furrowed as she regarded me. When she finished pouring the fourth and final cup, she stopped and leaned heartily onto the back of a chair with one elbow. "It's like anything else, in truth. If you've learned the ways, it's a straightforward task. Why do you worry over such menial things?"

"No reason to mention." I shook my head. "Naught but curiosity."

Quick rapping sounded on my door, and Dorynne skipped over to answer.

All three of my guests had arrived together. Before I went to welcome Nadia and my sisters, Mother Feathergale told me they'd be available in the serving room down the hall should we need anything else as we dined. She gave me a light hug and ushered Dorynne from the room.

"It smells fantastic," said Yasmynne.

Karynne came to me and dropped a light kiss on my forehead. "Yes, Mairynne, you've outdone yourself."

"The credit goes to my attendants. I merely watched as they prepared the table." I exchanged a smile with Nadia. "To have you all here tonight warms my heart. It's nice to be alone with my family. Come. Let us eat."

The earthy vegetable tarts were a delight, flaky crust melting on my tongue. Whatever ingredients went into the pastries outdid the juicy meat of the bird, but the two in combination made for a lovely flavor. I'd been hungrier than I'd known and said little as I took my fill.

When done, I turned to Yasmynne at my left. "How have you been, Sister?"

"I'm doing as well as can be expected. Nestryn has been a comfort." She nearly exploded from her seat as she added, "He plans to ask for Tsanseri's blessing whilst we're at the High Cloud Court for your ascension."

I sipped from my drink, wishing that I could be happier for my sister. "It does seem that the two of you have grown even closer since Father disappeared." I put on a smile, but as I'd never been one to mask my thoughts, my tone carried notes of all the worry and pressure I'd been facing.

Yasmynne shifted in her seat, her eyes flicking between us all.

"There's naught to worry over. In truth, I envy you and Nadia at having a partner to whom you may turn for consolation." I fidgeted with the knife at my plate's edge.

Everyone sat in silence until I changed the conversation's direction. "Anyway, since you mentioned the ascension, tell me. Are the plans nearing completion?"

"They are. We've sent invitations to the gnobles from each caste, and I received word from the Stone Singers earlier today that your crown is almost complete. I expect your first journal to arrive at the citadel from the Underhills tomorrow, just in time for the Triad to bless it before we depart for the High Cloud Court."

She had done her job well even though her motives lay elsewhere. At heart, she desired to gain an audience with Tsanseri, the Lady of Masks and the comtesse who regularly heard petitions in matters of courtly love. As for Karynne, her task had been closer to my heart's desire, and I turned to my right, giving my attention to her.

Without my asking, she began, "About Father's search party, Thalaj and I have arrived at a solid plan."

I had yet to share with my sisters that I'd only be assuming the leadership of our people on a temporary basis. Likewise, my ultimate intentions remained my own, so I hung on Karynne's every word, trying to weave together the final threads in my strategy.

She went on, "After we return from court, Thalaj will lead a team of only four to the marshes. Solarynne and Lukos have each named a junior member of their families who have agreed to make the journey, and the gensui has chosen someone from the guard, apparently a tracker he trusts implicitly."

A shadow of confusion passed over Karynne's face, but she dismissed whatever it had been with a roll of her shoulder and continued, "I'm uncertain why Thalaj believes that visiting the people of Umbra is a key to finding our father, but he insisted. As he has given our family only reasons to trust his judgment, I will defer and give him the room to guide the journey as he feels necessary."

Pressing my lips together, I nodded my satisfaction. I knew his reasons, but I knew him, too, and he likely had an ulterior reason or motivation to keep his information quiet. For my part, I had no desire to violate the trust he'd placed in me by sharing.

"Imrythel has nominated a messenger from the Sandsgale family to travel with the party so we may receive occasional word as to how the mission progresses," Karynne concluded her update.

Across the table, Nadia took the last bite of her tart, chewed, and swallowed. After a drink to wash it down, she said, "A messenger is a wonderful idea, don't you think, Mairynne?"

Our aunt seemed pleased that we were discussing the matter as a family, and though sending word through the messenger's network seemed a risk, I had little argument about the logic. It was a wise measure to ensure those who remained within Stormskeep would gain any significant information without having to wait for a traveling party to return and deliver the news. However, in truth, we didn't know what information they would find, and messengers tended to be voracious gossip mongers. Although I didn't voice concerns, my worry must have been clear in my expression.

Karynne rushed to add, "We will encode the messages. Only the search party will know the contents. A trusted messenger here at Stormskeep will decode it and deliver it to you and the royal advisory council."

She took a drink from her goblet. "Speaking of your council. Have you made your selections?" Karynne's insistence that I nominate my council and first advisor made me itch, but she was merely the loudest voice speaking of the shared expectation.

"I have," I answered easily, knowing that the council would not change as I'd be speaking only the temporary oath under the watchful eyes of Atun, Otarr, and Selene. I sighed. "It seems that everything is ready, despite that we should have been caring for our souls and mourning our mother. I suppose we have a duty to care for the Nantai in the wake of Father's disappearance as well.

"Sisters," I continued, "I thank you for spending this evening at my table. I'll let you go and attend to your own business. Tomorrow, we will release the nymphs, and the day following, we'll travel to the courts. I will ascend to the Serpentine Throne, and Yasmynne will gain a fiancé. Despite our losses, we can celebrate her betrothal."

When I stood, my sisters joined me. Yasmynne thanked me for the kind words, and we exchanged a warm, sisterly embrace.

Karynne kissed both my cheeks and smiled warmly. "You are proving to be wiser than your years, little sister."

Having put on the proper appearances for my sisters, I sighed my relief. My heart felt full in the moment of rare closeness. Maybe, given time, we'd regain some of the bonds we'd had as younglings. It would certainly go a long way to restoring a sense of normalcy, but my father's presence still called to me, and I had to answer that call first. Maybe my search would be fruitless, but at least I would be able to take comfort in the fact that I'd tried. Only then could I take the official oath and make my rule permanent.

As a group, we walked toward the door. After farewells, my sisters parted and I turned to Nadia. "Will you join me for a cordial before you leave?"

"Of course, darling."

"Thank you." I motioned to the room adjacent to the door. "One moment. I'll have Mother Feathergale heat a bottle and bring it to us on the veranda."

I stepped into the room where my attendants awaited and asked Mother Feathergale to prepare the cordials, then Nadia and I went to my small outdoor seating area where we could enjoy the sounds of falling water. A few minutes later, my newest attendant, Dorynne, appeared with two glasses of warmed fire-flower wine and placed them on the small table between our chairs.

"Thank you, Dorynne," I said.

She smiled and made her retreat.

Selene had assumed her night's watch in the skies, and with her came a chill. I lifted the glass and held it between my palms. Nadia watched me skeptically as she retrieved her own cordial. After the first sip, she let out a little *aah*. "Mairynne, why didn't you tell them you planned to take Morwyn's oath?"

"I'm not certain." I drank my warm and spicy red wine, then looked at her with a brow raised and a smirk. "Mayhap I am young, Nadia, but my father named me as his successor for a purpose. I hope you, unlike my sisters, don't believe tradition or expectation will so easily sway my mind."

She flashed a knowing smile. "As your mother always said, you have a will unlike any other."

The slightly reclined chair cradled me as I sank backward allowing the fiery wine to warm me from the inside out. Eyes closed, I enjoyed the sounds of Stormskeep and peace so easily found on this balcony overlooking the castle grounds, the residences, and markets below, and the walls that protected my people. With Nadia at my side, it felt as if some of my tension departed. I glanced over to see she had also found some ease or comfort in the quietness of twilight while sipping warmed ruby wine.

She rolled her head toward me and said, "The business with Thalaj and the search party still troubles you."

My aunt read me true. I had no desire for Thalaj to leave Stormskeep or for him to be away from me for however long the search might last, but his logic remained sound. The leader of the guard, with his time spent in the Unseen Guild, had the best and most unique qualifications over any other I could name.

As if they knew my thoughts, the tokens around my neck changed suddenly; a hot pulse flared against my chest. I reached for them. Certainly, that they'd come to me was a calling, and I felt equally sure that the sudden change was a further signal of that calling.

I would go. I had no idea how I'd convince Thalaj, and I knew the journey wouldn't be easy. Nevertheless, I would go.

Nadia spoke, pulling me from afar, "Maybe you should put away those reminders, Mairynne."

I shook my head, the twilit night coming back into focus. "The tokens trouble me, that is true, but how can I ignore them?" I searched her face, so like my mother's, for an answer she didn't have.

"You're about to accept a heavy duty, even if it's only a temporary one, to the Nantai people. Do not allow the past to distract you. You must trust that if King Atheryn lives, Thalaj will see him returned."

The ruby wine began to cool, and I finished what remained. Sitting forward, I gave her a warm smile. "It pleases me we've found a way to connect again, dear Aunt. I ask you though, is that what you would do if you were in my position? Sit by and wait."

"That isn't a choice I will ever face." She looked into her wine, finished it, and turned back to me. "So unfortunately, I cannot say."

Dorynne came from my rooms to retrieve the glasses and asked if there was anything else she could bring. As I watched her leave with empty goblets, I said, "I must choose a first advisor. My sisters once thought me naïve enough to choose Jessa."

Nadia pursed her lips, then asked, "Would it have been so bad? She was loyal and cared for you a great deal."

"Jessamyne Feathergale was my oldest and dearest friend. In the deepest part of her heart and much like her mother, she was little more than the sweetest of caregivers. She needed to grow up and find a partner to keep her safe, someone for her to nurture and give her younglings of her own to raise. She might have attended to my domestic needs for the remainder of her days and mine, but she would have never had the wisdom to offer advice on how I might best serve the Nantai people as their empress.

"And now someone has stolen the rest from her as well." I swallowed past a lump in my throat.

After some silent contemplation, Nadia suggested, "Solarynne would be a sensible selection."

"Ah, yes. She would." I answered. "For that matter, Lukos Thundergale would likely offer some prudent guidance for a young empress. However, I do not wish to unwittingly steal from my father's council. And I believe I need to add supporters of my interests. Then we have Karynne and Imrythel who suggested I choose a Sandsgale." I scoffed and looked over my shoulder.

Inside, behind where Nadia and I lounged, Dorynne and Mother Feathergale cleared the remnants of our evening's meal, the sounds of stacking dishes punctuating the ongoing notes of the Falls. I watched my aunt intently as gloaming turned to night and Selene's moon began to shine. As my mother's twin, Nadia had been around royal proceedings since my father married my mother. Her simple presence with Tennō Atheryn and Kōgō Noralynne, as well as my mother's continued work, had afforded my aunt much knowledge about the Nantai people, as well as the Small Folk. I leaned closer and scrutinized her closely. "As I have my own duty, I also have a duty to bestow upon you, dear Aunt."

FIVE

Into the High Cloud Court

THE SIXTIETH DAY OF mourning passed with my family standing on the fields that had hosted Kōgō Noralynne's funeral pyre and releasing the matured nymphs into the sky. All of Arashi gathered into the courtyard of Stormskeep, on the side closest to the fields. So many people had gathered, they had spilled out of the castle gates and filled the surrounding streets as they waited and watched. The cloud of slender nymphs rose, the nymphs fully transformed, lifting with their delicate iridescent wings to fill the sky and begin their journey into their next life. The final rite symbolized my mother's passing into her next life. Had she come to death naturally, the rite would have celebrated her life and released her into the empire beyond to take her rightful place with the Gods. Alas, with her life curtailed early, she would be reborn and walk amongst the Nantai people once again—or so was our belief.

The people drank and danced in the streets well into the dark hours, and on the morning after, we stored away our mourning clothes and looked toward happier times. For me, albeit sweet, the day also felt bitter. I'd endured enough mourning for a lifetime, but I had no time to grieve over the loss of Jessa as it was time to turn toward my other dilemma: rising to serve our people as political tradition demanded or following my heart and leaving the jewel city of Arashi behind in search of why the stones about my neck sang to me. Overnight, the High Cloud Court had moved into the sky above Stormskeep, and government affairs would dominate my immediate days ahead.

On the uppermost roof of Stormskeep Castle, alongside my father's counselors, my sisters and their first advisors, the Triad, Thalaj, and a few of his selected guardsmen, I awaited the arrival of the Cloud Courtiers to escort us into court. As the stairs coming down from the cloud formed in slow motion, I searched for Nadia and Corwyn, determined not to ascend into the courts without my first advisor at my side.

Karynne and Imrythel stood close, offering advice on how to handle myself while at the High Cloud Court.

"You should show only strength at all times," said Imrythel, an airy or haughty note to her words.

"Cloud Courtiers, illusionists that they are, will play games of deception," added Karynne.

Having been too young to attend the courts the last time my father had gone, I entered new territory that day along with having to accept the mantle of the people. I looked from my eldest sister to Yasmynne, who gave me a smile charged with excitement, then on to Thalaj. He stood to the side, stone-faced. Something about his at-ease manner told me he was anything but easy with this situation. To him, I dipped my head, acknowledging his tightly held concern, and I looked across the roof again for Nadia.

The billowing clouds met the roof's surface, and a group of eight courtiers descended two at a time, their shoulders held back and heads high, each more striking than the one before, yet all somehow alike. They, too, seemed to waft and curl and billow as they walked, and there were no features by which I could discern who might be who.

Imrythel leaned close to my ear and in her husky voice whispered, "The only way you will know a Cloud Courtier is by the emblem they wear on their shoulders. Each is unique, so as they introduce themselves, take note of their symbols."

Karynne said into my other ear, "Never forget, you are their empress, receiving your subjects. If you slip, they will take advantage."

The Cloud Courtier caste's opportunistic nature I felt well prepared to handle, but the resentment at my sister's need to constantly remind me of such things crawled beneath my skin. Her anger that Father had named me successor bled through in the sharp commands she disguised as advice. This situation weighed upon me, but as well as I knew the nature of the Cloud Courtiers, I knew Karynne's nature even better. Confronting her on that manner would do little to help, and in truth she might see it as an insult and retreat from our sisterhood all together. In this time, I couldn't afford to chase away someone who stood at my side in spite of her own umbrage.

The first two Cloud Courtiers approached, mist

swirling at their feet. Their skin glimmered as if someone had dusted it with a metallic powder, their lashes reminding me of branches after a snowstorm. The first one bowed in front of me. "A glorious morn to you and yours, my lady Mairynne Evangale. I am Cirro-Vior and my companion is Alto-Raal. I remember you as a youngling, and you have grown well into the Evangale charm."

Intrigued, I regarded the courtier, taking note of the crescent moon shape on the shoulder. Much must have shown on my face, because with the flourish of a hand, the image before me changed. I looked upon the visage of a boy, one whom I remembered, a boy I'd considered a friend and who visited our castle from time to time when I'd been a child. "Viordyn?" I asked.

His hand reversed the flourish and he returned to the glittering genderless apparition who'd been there before. "The one and only, Lady Mairynne," answered Cirro-Vior. "I have grown and gained my majority as have you. Are you and your council ready to ascend?"

My chest tightened at the word; the double meaning heavy on my soul. Scanning the rooftop again and not finding my aunt, I said, "We are not. I await one more. You will forgive the delay." I motioned to the clergy, beckoning.

Tasmynne answered my call, leaning in as I asked her to send an acolyte in search of my aunt.

In delicate silence, we waited.

When Nadia finally appeared, she didn't wear clothing appropriate for court. She hadn't combed her hair, and deep purple circles shadowed her eyes. She rushed over and threw her arms around me. "Mairynne, I am so very sorry." Her voice sounded broken and quivering in my ear.

When she pulled back, I could see tears threatening to overflow. She glanced furtively at the people who surrounded her, and her throat worked, but whatever had her so worked up had also stolen her words.

Solarynne Dawnsgale stepped forward from where the counselors stood and placed a gentle hand on my aunt's back. "What is it, Nadia? Will you tell us what has happened?"

Nadia shook her head and scrubbed at her face as the tears fell. When she collected herself enough to speak, she said, "It's Corwyn. He's very ill. He's been sick all night and is resting now. I have to get back. I'm sorry, Mairynne, but I cannot attend with you today."

"Nadia, it will be fine," I said, but wondered exactly how it would.

Solarynne said, "I'll come with you to care for him."

"No." My voice cracked on the harsh word, but I'd found my command. I hadn't intended to seem cold, but I had need of my supporters. "I, too, am sorry, Nadia. You may return to your partner, but I need Solarynne at my side. Tasmynne, you will send an acolyte to fetch the physicians and tend to Corwyn until we return." I raised my voice then, looking around at the stunned faces of Storm Sorcerers and Cloud Courtiers alike. "Everyone else will continue to the High Cloud Court as planned."

"Yes, Lady Mairynne." Tasmynne motioned over a young man and set him to the errand.

Solarynne turned a hard look to me as I made these decrees, but her eyes shone with her comprehension. She would attend to the duties she'd accepted by being part of the royal council.

I gave a single nod and hugged my aunt. "Go. See to your companion, and I'll do what I can here."

When she had departed, Lukos Thundergale stepped forward. "Lady Mairynne, if you'll allow, I can act as your first advisor for the purposes of ascension."

Solarynne's eyes dodged mine. Seeing further that she felt herself not up to the task, I accepted Lukos's offer and worked to suppress my worry over Corwyn—someone who'd been a part of my life for enough years that I considered him family, an uncle. I'd be just in deferring the meetings in light of an ill family member, but my presence there wouldn't help. Responsibility for Corwyn's recovery rested with our physicians.

With a deep breath and false confidence, I turned back to the Cloud Courtiers. I didn't relish the thought of accepting these responsibilities without Nadia at my side, but duty stood before me, a duty which I didn't intend to neglect that day. I am empress, I reminded myself, receiving my subjects.

To Cirro-Vior, I said, "We are ready."

As the procession went, a pair of the Cloud Courtiers led the way up the misty stairs. Thalaj and three of his soldiers followed, and I climbed somewhere in the middle with Lukos at my side. When we crested, arriving at the large yard before the series of castles in the clouds, my interim first advisor leaned in.

"The central castle is where the we hold Royal Court. The smaller courts are there to the right, the royal quarters to the left," he said.

Though I felt grateful for his guidance, I found myself more concerned with the courtiers present for our arrival and a sense of tension that erupted around the Stormskeep guards and Thalaj. As I watched, he stood rigidly with his feet apart and staggered. His hands crept toward the handles of his scimitynes. I rested a hand on Lukos's forearm and went toward the commotion.

Karynne and Imrythel fell into step beside me.

"What has happened?" I asked.

"Lady Mairynne," said Imrythel. "It seems that one of the courtiers has put your guards on alert with some ill words referring to their captain."

"Sister," Karynne added, "it would be best if you were the one to call halt to the matter."

In agreement, I moved faster, calling the wind to speed my step. When I arrived, one of the silver-dusted beauties spread arms wide and I caught the edge of the words. "But 'tis truth that you exist outside the castes, is it not? Blood of the highest order contaminated by the fourth would traditionally be offered up to the Tsinti, is that not so?"

"Enough!" I snapped.

Silence fell again, and all eyes turned. Thalaj shot me a warning look, making his desire that I remain uninvolved clear. Though I also detected an exacerbation, suggesting what he wouldn't voice: I told you as much.

Breathing slowly to manage my nerves, I reminded myself, I am empress, receiving my subjects. To the offender, I said, "May I have your name?"

The Cloud Courtier turned to me and sank into a bow. "I am called Alto-Trea, my lady Mairynne."

Otherwise indiscernible, the emblem on the courtier's shoulder became a calling card. It showed a pattern of wispy swirls, resembling lines of the black swans that swam in the pool at the foot of Sundai Falls.

The swan, I decided, and wondered again why they all chose to look so similar. Lifting my chin, I said, "Were you familiar, Alto-Trea, with Kōgō Noralynne's work for the Nantai people, that she worked across castes and with the Small Folk alike, and that she believed all deserve an equal voice?"

I feigned a pause as if to await a reply, but before anyone could make a sound, I continued, "Before you answer, I am certain you are." I smiled, having claimed the upper hand. "As I am my mother's daughter, I shall not tolerate words, no matter how gently spoken, that slander. Is that abundantly clear?"

This time I allowed the courtier to answer.

The swan bent at the waist. "As you command, Lady Mairynne." And for all I could discern, the courtier held no emotion or reaction to my order. If animosity existed within, the swan contained it well.

In reality, amidst those gathered, every Cloud Courtier's face seemed solemn, identical. As for the faces of the Storm Sorcerers in attendance, each told a different story, but all seemed proud of the stance I'd taken. Karynne outright smiled, and Imrythel nodded once with her approval. Despite the vote of confidence, I was ready to be out of the spotlight if only for a brief time.

"Now," I started, "I understand the first of our proceedings will be this evening. I'd like to freshen up before then. Alto-Trea, as you have so eagerly welcomed my party, you will kindly show us to the royal quarters." I held the swan's icy gaze.

"Naturally, Lady Mairynne."

The courtier's manner remained poised, and I still perceived no emotion as we followed. The feeling was like nothing I'd ever experienced. It was as if I were dealing with animated dolls. Hopefully Lukos would have some wise counsel as we took repast for the afternoon. I understood now that I'd met Cloud Courtiers before, but my past experience with the person I'd known as Viordyn had failed to prepare me for this.

Inside the royal chambers, Lukos thanked Alto-Trea and closed us inside, away from the courtiers. Our rooms provided ample space for all in attendance, private apartments surrounding a common area for meals and meetings. Walls, floors, even the furniture and linens in light blues, silvers, and whites reflected light and added to the feeling of being in the clouds. I stepped to the balcony, and far below, Stormskeep drifted away as we rose into the sky. Under my feet, I hadn't noticed the movement, the Cloud Court had already departed its dock. I ran a hand over a stone wall, amazed at how cloud magic made such a solid structure lighter than air.

A throat cleared at the door and I turned to find Thalaj casually leaning to one side at the threshold.

"Join me," I said, "and close the door behind you."

"Your display back there was unnecessary."

"I disagree."

He smiled, a glint in his eyes saying that mayhap he enjoyed my disagreement by some measure.

As the soon-to-be empress, I owed no explanation. But within, a need to voice my reasons drove my agitated speech. "That was their first interaction with me as their empress. There wasn't room for leniency. What was said before I arrived?"

The spark in his eyes went dark. "That, I'll not repeat. You heard enough to get the courtier's point." He crossed over and leaned on the railing, taking in the scene below, the Stormskeep castle, falls, citadel, and city surrounded by the high wall. "It looks small from here."

"That it does. Home is a wonderous place," I said idly, resisting the urge to press him more. I had gained their meaning well enough, and hopefully my stance resonated strongly enough.

"You will be back there soon, as Kōgō Mairynne Evangale."

I looked into the distance, where the fields and forests spread across Nantai, wondering where our travels would one day take us. Feeling distant myself, I ignored the honorific and said, "For a time." Then, returning to the present and hardening my resolve, I added, "Thalaj, when I have concluded my business at court, I intend to come with you to find my father."

◇◇◇◇◇◇◇◇◇◇◇◇◇◇◇◇

ONCE MY FATHER'S AND now my protector, Thalaj dropped his shoulders on a sigh, his eyes shifting in an obvious search for the right response. All of his training, every instinct he'd honed to perfection, and his very foundation of being, I had just called into question with my announcement. For all his tactical agility and gallantry, he struggled when facing a proposal with which he disagreed. Mayhap the hesitation hailed from his protective nature. Maybe he felt inadequate given his intermingled bloodlines. The former, I could do little to change. The later, I would one day see handled, but not while my father lived and could still rule the Nantai people. For now, I watched. And waited for his reply. If my plight resulted in success, I'd beg for the decree from the restored emperor. Until then, I had to believe he would grant his youngest daughter's wish.

When Thalaj's reply came, it sounded as assured as

if he'd known what he'd say all along. "Lady Mairynne, I am no royal advisor. I have no political knowledge, nor have I an agenda. Combat and covert endeavors are where I excel, and this is no mission for someone born to rule the Nantai people. I beg of you to trust that, if he lives, I will find Tennō Atheryn and return him safely to you at Stormskeep."

I reached for my necklace. His words struck me and, had it not been for the burning stone against my skin, I may have heeded his wisdom. "Thalaj," I said, placing my free hand on his forearm. "This has little to do with how well I trust you to return my father." I gave a single laugh freely toward the sky at how, in reality, I trusted him more than any other person. With a smile, I added, "That you will be at my side gives me the confidence to make the journey."

He pressed his lips tighter. Then quietly, he said "I can't take you to Umbra." Glancing toward the door and lowering his voice even more, he went on, "In confidence, I had planned to enter the Evernight Marshes alone. Avoiding the enchantments there requires too much concentration for me to watch over another. Especially you."

"Wha—" I began, but he'd stopped my objection before it had really begun. The fact that he'd planned to do this all on his own despite the guise of taking a team brought me up short. After a pause to gather my own thoughts, I asked, "But you will return to Stormskeep after, with the totem?"

"I will."

"And how do you propose to convince the Small Folk at Evernight's heart to part with something so prized?"

Thalaj remained silent, telling me no more about

what tactics he might use, but by his silence also that he would bring back the totem at any cost. Of that, I felt assured, and I believed it with as much certainty as I had faith that my father still lived. Whatever he planned didn't leave me feeling easy, but it sufficed, allowing me to imagine the result would be worth the cost and that no one would come to harm in obtaining this relic.

The door creaked and Lukos stood in the frame, tall, slender, with hands folded in front of him. "Lady Mairynne, your attendants and your . . . sister have arrived." His lip curled and he hesitated on the word *sister* like it tasted wrong in his mouth.

The feeling seemed typical of the counselor. Yasmynne's exuberance scrubbed his cool composure like little else could manage.

"Thank you, Lukos," I said. My gaze flitted back to Thalaj. "This is not the end of our conversation."

He tipped his head forward, then stood straight and said, "My team should have searched your rooms for any dangers by now. We will help with the chests, then wait in the outer rooms if you should have need of us."

He passed Lukos, turning to slide through the tight doorway. Lukos stepped aside but remained square and kept his attention on me—a tension or possible distaste that I hadn't noticed before. With the exception of Ohmyn Havengale, my counselors each worked hard to disguise their thoughts and offer advice when needed, but as I spent more time with them, I learned and took note of what their body language said that their words did not. I had little desire to stir conflict within my own retinue here, away from our home, so I allowed the slight to pass. Lukos turned as I went inside.

My counselors gathered around a table while

Dorynne, Thalaj, and his small team moved our chests of clothing on the wind to each of the chambers. Mother Feathergale was in the process of greeting my sister. Karynne stooped to return the embrace and did so eagerly, greeting the woman who had attended to all of us as children. After they parted, the small but lithe woman came to me with open arms.

"You seem a bit out of breath," I said as we hugged.

She smiled and flipped a hand dismissively. "The air's thinner. Takes more effort to gather the wind for moving around the heavies. But don't you worry; we'll get everything settled. You go about your business."

When she moved away, Yasmynne appeared in her place, placing both hands on my shoulders. "Mairynne, Nestryn and I will visit Comtesse Tsanseri's court on the morrow. She has asked that we bring witnesses to vouch for us. Will you come?" She looked nervously between her betrothed and me.

My brow felt heavy, not from my sister's request, but at the realization that the Cloud Courtier went by *Tsanseri* rather than one of the factions. Though I wasn't sure there was sufficient time on the morrow, I wanted to serve my sister's wishes. I put on a smile and answered, "Of course, Yasmynne."

To Lukos, I asked, "Tsanseri is a Cloud Courtier, true?"

"She is."

"How is it we know she is *she*?" I asked, still wondering at my next question regarding the factions.

"Comtesse Tsanseri always chooses a feminine form. She believes it better represents all the gentle things about love and affection."

"Oh, Lukos," Azurynne Nightingale admonished, "you know there is more substance to it than that."

I turned to her, brows raised and waiting to hear more about this *more.*

She continued, "Tsanseri believes herself better than the uniform ways of the Cloud Courtiers. Her given name is Cirro-Tsan, but when she began the proceedings of Love's Court, she dispensed with the faction naming, as well as with the same illusions as the rest of the courtiers."

"But do not let that fool you, Mairynne," Imrythel interjected. "People across Nantai call her Comtesse of the Masque for good reason." She arched a black brow over one glinting green eye.

Lukos cleared his throat and said, "You will know her by her seat at the center of court. I do believe it is wise for you to visit her court whilst you are here, and as we must travel to the seats of the each of the other gnobles before ascension, tomorrow is satisfactory."

Turning back to my acting first advisor, I asked, "How long will gathering the gnobles take?"

He folded his hands behind his back and paced as he answered, "Traveling by cloud is the quickest route, but it will still take a handful of days to make the circuit to the Iced Plains in the north, Kōdaina Kori, the desert's edge, and finally to the Barrows."

My hand found the stones around my neck. Hot and cold. The cold one burned this time as I spoke, "Tell me, Lukos, or anyone. Solarynne . . ."

She surfaced from her daze and turned to me, but waited.

" . . . or Azurynne, or Ohmyn, why have we not

invited the Small Folk or the Tsinti to the proceedings of the realm? Should not all have a seat on the high council? And who will speak for the casteless?"

Ohmyn gasped, a shaky hand covering his mouth. Azurynne and Lukos had mirrored expressions, pressing their lips together in an attempt to measure their words.

Solarynne stood and circled the table toward me. "I am sorry, Mairynne, that I have been wearing my worry over Corwyn and offering you little counsel. In this matter, though, even your mother, Kōgō Noralynne, had trouble finding or convincing any of those peoples to join us."

Lukos found his voice again. "The Tsinti live apart from the rest of the Nantai people. We have never been able to locate them at will."

Azurynne snapped, "And the Small Folk ward their seats of power heavily. It's too dangerous to try to approach them. And they refuse meetings with us to discuss such matters." She threw a hand up in the air and asked, "Bless the Triad, when was the last time we received any of the Small Folk at Stormskeep?"

I looked at her hard. "I have noted your point, Azurynne. Albeit I cannot recall the last time a Cloud Courtier, Fire Forger, Frost Fighter, Stone Singer, or Underhill Dweller visited our keep."

She shrank under my stare.

"Karynne," I said. "Would you go to the outer rooms and ask Thalaj to return?"

When he appeared before me, my first guardsman bowed, stood, and awaited the reason for my summons.

"Gensui Thalaj," I said, "When you travel to the Small Folk of Umbra, you will deliver a message on behalf of the empress. That should be me by the time your meeting comes to pass." Swallowing the sudden lump in my throat, I asked him to extend an open invitation to the leader who held Umbra's seat.

When he agreed, I turned my attention to more immediate matters. "Now, can someone tell me how to best deal with the oddities of these courtiers?"

Ohmyn scoffed, then gave a hearty laugh. "Lady Mairynne, if you think the courtiers are your only concern, wait until you meet the other castes who will attend the High Cloud Court of Gnobles. These proceedings are, shall we say, quite colorful." He lifted a mug from the table, drinking deeply with a trail of foam drizzling down his chin.

Regarding my rotund counselor, I gnawed at the inside of my lip. At length, I gave a rueful smile, deciding to credit Ohmyn for that bit of wisdom. "Well," I said, "from my small experience today, it certainly seems that what I have learned of the Nantai peoples in theory may not have been adequate preparation."

◇◇◇◇◇◇◇◇◇◇◇◇◇◇◇◇

OF THOSE WHO ATTENDED court on my behalf, only Thalaj agreed to be at my side for Nestryn and Yasmynne's assignation at Love's Court. My counselors had old acquaintances they wished to see or things they wished to buy from the cloud markets. Or, in Solarynne's case, she wished to remain in solitude and offer prayer to Selene that her brother would be well. Edamyn, priest of Atun, spoke for the Triad in haughtily stating that neither Gods nor clergy attended such proceedings and excused himself, Tasmynne, and Arlyn; they would retire to Otarr's temple until the ascension ceremony itself.

Two Cloud Courtiers greeted us upon our arrival at

Comtesse Tsanseri's court. They invited Nestryn alone into court and directed Yasmynne, Thalaj, and me to wait in the anteroom which turned out to be an open-air seating area with several ornately designed settees, each wide enough to seat two in close proximity. Mist floated at our feet, obscuring the floor. When the courtiers had left us alone, Yasmynne sank slowly onto the closest sofa, looking ghostly and wringing her hands.

I went to my sister, laid a hand on her shoulder, and said, "You've no need to worry. Nestryn loves you greatly, and he will show that to the Comtesse."

"But Mairynne, why wouldn't she receive us together, as a couple?" Her brows peaked as she searched my face for an answer that I could only wish to possess.

I shrugged one shoulder but found it hard to hold eye contact when I could offer little to soothe her fears. "There is little we can do but wait and see."

Thalaj waited for me to sit, then took the place at my side. His solemn look bespoke naught of his thoughts, and the three of us remained in silence for quite some time until worries began to grow in my thoughts as well. Curious about what awaited behind the silver-scrollwork doors, I whispered to Thalaj, "Have you been to this court before?"

"I have not." He shook his head slowly.

"What do you know of the Comtesse Tsanseri?" I asked.

"Very little, Lady Mairynne." He adjusted in his seat, moving one scabbard so he could face me better. "My guidance would be to remain open and calm. Observe and listen. If there is something I have learned of people over the years, it is to trust slowly. You never know where you might find an ally . . . or an adversary."

The advice embodied the man at my side, and it seemed my best course of action. I vowed to try to do the same, not only at Tsanseri's court, but for the remainder of our time in the High Cloud Courts. Time passed, and I made small talk with Yasmynne as a means to distract her while we awaited summons. After maybe an hour, the doors opened.

At last, Nestryn exited alone through the silvery door. The Cloud Courtiers standing to either side remained statuesque. Yasmynne stood as he went to her and bowed to one knee, taking her hand in his. "My love and shining light," he started. "I want you day and night."

I rolled my eyes and looked at Thalaj, trying not to laugh at the horrid attempt at poetry. A muscle jumped in my guard's jaw, and his eyes widened ever so slightly. Yasmynne, conversely, looked lovingly upon the man at her feet. Inhaling deeply, I reminded myself, open and calm, observe and listen, and I worked to keep my expression neutral.

"The Comtesse has given me her instruction and now bids that you appear before her. May I escort you, my lady Yasmynne Evangale?"

My sister grinned at me, barely containing excitement that begged for freedom, then back to Nestryn, she said, "Of course."

Nestryn added, "Comtesse Tsanseri asked that you bring the witnesses before her." He stood and turned expectantly to Thalaj and me. "Will you both join us?"

I held out a hand. "Please, lead the way."

Thalaj offered me an arm, his brow raised in question.

"Observe?" I asked, placing my hand on his forearm.

"And listen," he answered.

The courtiers at the doors pulled them wide and we followed the cheerful couple inside. Unlike the royal chambers' decor and in contrast with the whites, silvers, and airy blues that colored the rest of the High Cloud Courts, vibrant color painted the interior of Tsanseri's court—tapestries of red and gold, lively paintings, upholstery in whimsical teal or purple, and silks of yellow and orange. Much smaller than I had expected, the room smelled of incense and spice. Several artists with easels and paints took positions along the outskirts of the room, readying their supplies to capture the scene. Unattended musical instruments rested against the walls.

In the place of chairs, pillows lay in a circle, and the person who could only be Tsanseri sat on the largest at the far side, with her legs folded and hands palms up on each knee. Her auburn hair flowed in abundant waves and her skin seemed dusted with gold rather than silver. She smiled serenely, welcoming us to her court.

Two courtiers sat to her left and two to her right, all taking a similar feminine form and posed to mirror their leader. One of the four said, "Comtesse Tsanseri welcomes petitioner, Lady Yasmynne Evangale, and the man who wishes her hand to the center of our circle."

Another said, "Likewise, the witnesses, future Kōgō Mairynne Evangale and Gensui Thalaj Northerngale, honor Love's Court with their presence."

My heart flopped in my chest. I sorely desired to rebut the title, but I dared not. Not yet.

Comtess Tsanseri then spoke with a mischievous gleam in her eye and a smirk. "Please, do make yourselves comfortable, and let us enjoy this part of our day." To the courtiers who had allowed us inside, she called, "Bring the artists and musicians, and bring sparkling wine for each of our guests."

Yasmynne sat in the center of the circle on a lush pillow, Nestryn on the rug at her side. As other courtiers began to filter in and take up instruments or paint brushes, Thalaj and I each knelt on pillows to one side so we could see Tsanseri beyond my sister. A courtier appeared, offering a fluted glass filled with a glittery, bubbly wine. After I received mine, she handed the next one to Thalaj.

With alacrity, he accepted but held it before him without a taste. I tipped mine, only enough to wet my tongue, and widened my eyes. Sweet and cool, it tingled in my mouth. Not knowing its possible effects, I then chose to act as Thalaj and hold the glass without partaking.

Comtesse Tsanseri raised her hands. "Shall we begin?"

A commotion, agreement, clapping, and small cheers went up around the room. Tsanseri nodded to her left, then right. The musicians began gently playing flutes and strings. With the ambiance established, the Comtesse focused her attention on my sister. "Lady Yasmynne, what has this lowly man done to deserve your affection?"

Yasmynne held her chin high. "Comtesse, Nestryn began courting me before my mother passed." She looked in my direction with a slight smile, then returned her gaze toward the mistress of the court. "My sisters have always said that I have much need of affection, more so than anyone. Nestryn has provided that affection throughout the mourning period."

"Future Kōgō Mairynne, do you approve of this betrothal?"

Her address took me off guard, and I faltered but

recovered quickly with truth. "Comtesse Tsanseri, I want naught but happiness for my sister, and I have seen that Nestryn makes her so. I will give my blessing," I answered.

"Has he brought you gifts?" she asked of my sister.

"He brings me the gift of holding me, of calming my heart and soul, of being close to me when I am in need, and of caring for me as no other can," my sister said, but her head tilted slightly.

I couldn't see her face, but I imagined it confused. Our traditions of courtship at Stormskeep involved little in the way of gifting, but everyone from the Syrensea to the neighboring nation of Yōtei had heard rumors of how Tsanseri was the true authority on love. I knew in my heart that the reason we sat in the rainbow-colored room was simply because Yasmynne craved validation.

Tsanseri said, "For a love to be fine, your suitor should bring you gifts, and many gifts at that. Has he written you poetry or letters?"

Quietly, Yasmynne said, "He has not, but—"

The Comtesse held up a hand to silence her rebuttal. "These are the foundations of fine love, my lady. How is it you seek my blessing without your betrothed having attended to these most basic of matters?"

As my sister explained their ongoing relations to her self-appointed judge and jury, I uncomfortably felt the pressure of eyes upon me. Losing track of the official conversation, I scanned the room, attempting to discern between the people who all looked the same or to see the emblem worn on their left shoulder. A violinist, rapt in her work, leaned to one side then the other as she worked the bow. A painter studied Tsanseri and dabbled on the canvas. Most were engaged in their current creations, but at length, I found the source of my discomfort. Across the room, a courtier stared harshly at me and Thalaj. She, for the courtiers had all assumed an air of femininity presumably for Tsanseri's good graces, stood angled just enough that I could see the emblem on her shoulder.

A swan.

Alto-Trea.

Almost everything about the courtier appeared differently from only a day before, but that emblem marked her. And her stare carried too much disdain to obscure the true person. I leaned toward Thalaj and said, "Remember Alto-Trea from our arrival?"

He nodded, but confusion tugged his brows together as he peered over to the new image across the court.

"It's pretty clear that the swan will be a hard-won ally," I whispered, "if not already an adversary."

By way of reply, he said, "As of yet, I would count Alto-Trea as neither ally nor adversary. It is hard to know based on a person's prejudices. Some of your counselors hold that very same prejudice." Thalaj, though he believed himself inadequate as more than a guard, once again offered an acute observation.

Rendered silent, I stared off with Alto-Trea across the room. The courtier broke eye contact first when Tsanseri clapped three times to call the room's attention.

Once silence had descended, Tsanseri made her judgment. "I have heard Nestryn's case for your hand, but this joining has not yet developed sufficiently to deserve blessing from Love's Court. For one year, one month, one week, and one day, Nestryn must practice the ways of fine love. You, Lady Yasmynne, will keep his gifts, his letters, his poems, and any art he makes in dedication to you. After this period, you will present a sampling of his finest efforts at this court." She paused for some minor sounds of approval to pass. "Then, and only then, will I be able to bless your union."

Outside, I stood with Thalaj and breathed in the unperfumed air, allowing Otarr to shine on my face for long warm moments. I remained uncertain about that in which I had just partaken, but two things seemed clearer than before. Tsanseri held a power over many of the Cloud Courtiers that I couldn't describe, one that encouraged them to disguise themselves to her liking alone. And, secondly, I needed more information about Alto-Trea.

Yasmynne and Nestryn joined us, and I turned to my sister. Putting on a jovial smile in hopes of lightening her spirits, I said, "So, it seems we will have a wedding after a year, month, week, and day?"

She returned only a thin smile. "It all just appears to be so much work, Mairynne," she said with a note of rejection.

I nudged my sister at the thought. "Nay, Nestryn has stood beside you through mourning our mother. We can all see the love he showers on you. This trial will be naught for him, and you will be increasingly happy as he gives you more and more affection with each offering Tsanseri has prescribed."

Yasmynne took Nestryn's hand in both of hers. Looking from him back to me, she said, "I suppose you speak the truth. I had just hoped that we could wed sooner."

Hugging myself about the waist, I said, "I, for one, am happy for you both. And this will give you ample time to plan for a ceremony to outshine all weddings that have gone before."

That thought brought a shining light into her eyes, and she clasped me into a tight hug. I squeezed her back, hoping that it would be long enough that I would return with Father and that he would be able to see his daughter married properly under the Triad.

SIX

Ascension

THE COLD DISTURBED MY sleep almost as much as the ascension ceremony scheduled to begin at midday. Arising from my bed, I went to the wardrobe and found a heavy cloak. Though I wore a long woolen gown to sleep and the blankets were heavy, the change in temperatures, certainly attributable to the current location of the High Cloud Court, chilled my fingers so much that they felt thin and ached. After I had tied the heavy cloak at my waist, I rubbed the numb end of my nose and paced the room, my chest squeezing tighter with every step. When I all but couldn't breathe, I went to the balcony and looked off into the night. We had descended, and under Selene, the land just beyond the clouds' edges appeared silver.

With slippered feet, I left my chamber, easing the door closed behind me so as to not disturb those who still slept in other areas of the royal suite. I thought the large, manicured lands around the courts would be quiet at this time and anticipated I could walk alone under the stars that guarded the night.

"Venturing out alone?" My oldest sister's voice, like a resting storm rolling in from a distance, halted me in my tracks. She strolled toward me, also wearing her heavy cloak. "I couldn't sleep. It seems you're having the same troubles."

I nodded, looking between her and the door.

She extended a hand. "Mind if I join you? You, of all people, really shouldn't be about at night on your own."

"Is there some danger I'm unaware of?"

"I wouldn't name it danger, but who knows what agendas lie among the castes. Now we have arrived at our last stop before the ceremonies, it's likely that you won't be alone even if you should leave these chambers that way."

Even though I knew ascension would commence at midday, I hadn't kept track of where we were in our journey. "Who joins us this night?"

"Gnoble Brimr, his wife, Svarta, and any other Underhill Dwellers they choose to bring to court." Karynne looked around the dark room, then back to me and smiled. "Did you have a destination? Or simply planning to wander?"

My brows felt heavy as I considered. "I only considered being outside, away from the confines of these rooms."

"Will you allow my company?"

"I will."

"Then why are we waiting?"

Having no answer, I shrugged and pulled the door open. Outside, the temperature had fallen, and I pulled the hood over my head.

Karynne hugged her cloak tighter. "'Tis cold near the Iced Plains," she said, her breath fogging the night.

Slowly, we strolled through the halls and out into the night where silver mists rolled, parting in front of us and circling in our wake. There, on an island in the clouds, little extra space did not allow for long walks out of doors; and on that quiet night, I desired the park near the River Sundai, where the waters fell from the cliffs and began the journey toward the Syrensea. It was in this silent, moon-clad moment, that I understood how much anxiety had gathered under my skin due to the absent sound of rushing water. That night, I wanted my home more than anything, but several days still remained before I'd step foot in Stormskeep once again.

To our right, a wide, trellis-covered corridor stretched to the edge of the cloud island. Under Otarr's bright eye, the markets pulsed there, merchants trading for various wares from throughout Nantai and beyond. Others had returned with everything from practical wares wrought by the Stone Singers to strands of reddish pearls from the Copper Coast to spices and minerals collected from the Great Sands Desert. Seeing their prizes, I wished for the freedom to trade rather than learning about the gnobles and how my ascension ceremony might play out.

Looking down briefly, I asked Karynne, "Where is Imrythel this evening?"

"I imagine she sleeps like everyone else."

"With the exception of the dinner in my rooms, I think this might be the first time I've seen you without her at your side since Mother's death."

"That is only in Otarr's hours. I see you little in the evenings," she accused.

We meandered on in silence for several more moments toward the courtyard where we'd first embarked onto the High Cloud Courts. My sister took her turn in breaking the silence. "Tsanseri's decision tossed our dear sister into quite the state of agitation, don't you agree?"

I laughed lightly. "Comtesse Tsanseri has a strict idea of how a courtier should treat the woman he courts."

"Aah, yes. That's similar to what Yasmynne said. Only she ranted for a good time over the matter."

"She was quite dejected afterward," I said.

Karynne rushed to add, "But I think she is becoming more and more fond of the idea with each passing moment."

"Is that not what you'd expect, Sister?" I faced to her with a questioning gaze.

She angled herself toward the light so I could see her expression fill with sheer amusement. "I find it, shall we say, an apropos happenstance that she feels forced into something she'll love, yet she can't see its value. Love seems to blind."

Those last words grated, but her expression remained open and insinuated mere observation. She took my hands in hers and went on, "Mairynne, I must apologize." Her brows furrowed and she pursed her lips.

Curious, I waited for her to continue, my eyes wide and blinking, but words escaping me. Mayhap I found myself the slightest bit bewildered that my ever-so-poised and in-command sister offered an apology so readily.

"I admit," she said with a chuckle. "I was bitter when Father wrote you into the annals as his successor. It should have been me by birthright, but that is only part of our ways. I've spent too much time worrying over that. I want . . ." She swallowed hard, struggling to get out something that had clearly weighed on her heart. "No, that's not right. I need for us to be closer again. Like we were when we were children, when we sat at Father's feet listening to the stories of the realm." She squeezed my hand, and when her eyes met mine, they glistened.

Grasping her hand tighter in return, I sighed. "Oh Kahry, despite the cold of this night, that warms my soul." I wrapped my arms around my sister, and she pulled me close. We stood there in an embrace at the edge of the only courtyard on the island, reconnecting.

"You haven't called me that in many years." When we parted, she said, "It's taken me a long while to understand the kind of sister I need to be. I only want the best for the Nantai people, and I need to help you make that happen, to be the best sister I can. Like Nadia was to Mother. I'm sorry I haven't been there for you like that before." Tears pooled in her eyes, reflecting Selene's light.

I welcomed having her back at my side. "But you're here now. That's really all that matters." So easily I forgave, because in my heart and soul, I wanted this too.

A metallic clang and thud sounded across the yard, echoing from the stone faces of the castle buildings. Karynne and I both pivoted toward the noise, and I held my breath as we tried to make out the figures moving in the distance. In my periphery, Karynne's posture eased.

"Should we go meet Gnoble Brimr?" she asked.

∞∞∞∞∞∞∞∞∞∞∞∞∞

ONE OF THE CLOUD Courtiers caught sight of us before we arrived and met us a dozen paces out. When close enough, I could make out the crescent moon shape embroidered onto the shoulder. "Cirro-Vior, good eve to you," I said with my chin held high.

The courtier bent at the waist, one arm wrapped around the front of the waist and the other around the back. Standing, Cirro-Vior greeted us and asked, "What brings you out in the hours between?"

Glancing to Karynne and back to the courtier, I said, "We could ask the same of you."

"Lady Mairynne, the Underhill Dwellers have an intolerance for the light from Otarr. They always embark under Selene's silver light. As I have charge of receiving the High Court's guests, I am here to welcome Gnoble Brimr from the Barrows."

"If I may, Viordyn?" I began.

Almost imperceptibly, but still, the courtier bristled.

"I'm sorry." I smiled. "Cirro-Vior. Would you be so kind as to introduce us to the gnoble and his wife? Aah . . ."

"Svarta," Karynne added helpfully.

Cirro-Vior nodded. "Naturally, Lady Mairynne."

The tales of the Underhill Dwellers did these people few favors, but they also did little to depict their true image. They were a stout people who stood a head shorter than the average Storm Sorcerer but from a hunched posture rather than shortened spine. I, being shorter than most Storm Sorcerers, still needed to gaze down to greet the gnoble and his wife. Under Selene's light, their skin and hair were both so pale they seemed gray.

As the courtier called to Gnoble Brimr, the Underhill Dweller turned, and I stifled a gasp at the oddity that stared back at me. He had a wide forehead and oversized ears that each came to three subtle points. Eyes that gave off a warm yellow light regarded me. His eyebrows and mustache extended toward his sides and appeared to be something other than hair—thicker and fingerlike. I made note to inquire about that later. He loped over and extended an arm that at resting hung to his knees. His wide hand with blunt nails awaited my acceptance.

When I accepted, he folded the chunky fingers around mine, and though I'd never considered my hands dainty, they seemed wispy in comparison to his.

Brimr smiled and his mustache seemed to move of its own accord, for the person himself hadn't budged. His voice, when he spoke, was gravelly. "Lady Mairynne, I see. You have the look and feel of Kōgō Noralynne. We are pleased to know you. We have brought the journal that will be the first of your annals, as well as other papers and scrolls as gifts to the newly ascended empress and her people." He turned away briefly to yell, "Svarta! Come."

My stomach twisted into knots at the mention of Mother's name, and the icy stone resting on my chest flared. I forced my hands to remain at my sides and keep my mind with the newcomers. Mother had passed into her next life, the mourning period had passed, and I needed to tend to our realm's business.

To my continued surprise, Svarta resembled her husband in most features. The main differences between the two were in breadth, her more delicate lips beneath a mustache, and two brown bands that ran down from under her ears, down her neck, and disappeared beneath the line of her dress. Svarta had voluminous, curly white hair that hung over one shoulder, and she wore a trio of piercings in each point of her earlobes.

I held out my hand to Brimr's wife with a smile. "It is lovely to meet you, Gnoble Lady Svarta."

After she shook my hand, Brimr wrapped an arm around her waist and gruffly pulled her to him. "My wife," he said to her, "after tomorrow, this will be our new empress."

Svarta's eyes flashed, then dimmed. She reached into a pocket and brought out a compact package. Grabbing one of my hands, she placed it in my palm and folded my fingers closed, backing away with a slight smile and twitch of her mustache. She looked at Brimr and made a few clicking noises while her mustache danced.

Brimr grinned proudly and said, "It's one of the best tubers grown by my people. A delicacy. My wife believes you will be a fine empress."

"Thank you, Svarta. I appreciate your confidence," I said, though I couldn't fathom what gave her that impression upon first sight.

Karynne leaned over and whispered in my ear. "You only have a few hours left to sleep before morning."

I nodded, straightened, and said, "I am happy to have met you both, but I should return and sleep. Until tomorrow."

We went, my heart heavy at all the talk of Mother and feeling somewhat alone without Nadia here to support me. The apology from Karynne had taken me by surprise but felt sincere and difficult for her. For me, it was long overdue. I decided on that walk back to our rooms that if she could extend herself, then I should too.

"Kahry," I said as we meandered back beyond the market.

She made a small sound of assent.

I continued, "Tomorrow, the oath I will take will not be the permanent oath of ascension."

Karynne grasped my arm and pulled me to a stop, facing her. "What do you mean, Sister?"

With a look into the market alley and one down the hall before us, it appeared we were alone, so I told her about my plan. "I will open with the words of Tennō Makenyn from the first of the annals just before he underwent the separation from the Kuroidragon. His annals read, 'I shan't wholly relinquish my right to rule the people. Before I undergo the extraction, my brother Morwyn shall take this oath and rule in my stead until I am once again able.' " After a pause, I added, "Tomorrow, I will take Morwyn's oath."

"Mairynne, what are you talking about? Do you think this will appease the Council? The Triad?"

"I don't know, Kahry, but—"

She held up a hand. "I know, you feel Father lives. You've said so enough times."

I searched her eyes for understanding, and I believed I found it. "It's also that I am not ready to be empress." I looked down. "I'm scared, Kahry." As of yet, I didn't know if I could trust my sister enough to tell her I planned to go with Thalaj. That would stir another series of questions I had no intent of answering on that night.

"Mairynne, you must inform the counselors of your intentions before we go into court tomorrow. You can't afford dissension within the Storm Sorcerers caste at High Cloud Court. If there are indeed any castes intent on unseating us as the first caste, it would open the door wider for them to step inside."

"There is no time to discuss this with the advisors, Karynne. Nadia and Solarynne already know. After ascension tomorrow, everyone will know, and I don't think our father's counselors will openly show dissent.

Will you keep this between us until that time, Sister?"

She started to speak but, seemingly at a loss for words, pressed her mouth into a tight line. Maybe she only thought better of objecting as we were finally making peace. Which was the case, I couldn't say.

I didn't ask.

Rather, I inquired quietly, "Do you think it's the right thing?"

"It is not a course I would take." She looked at me long and hard. For what she searched, I was unsure. What she found, I also did not know, but she finally said with a reluctant smile, "I will keep it between us. And I do think it right. You must follow your soul's calling and be true to thine self first. Wasn't that the lesson Father always taught?"

◇◇◇◇◇◇◇◇◇◇◇◇◇◇◇◇

BY MIDDAY WHEN MY ascension began, the cloud island had risen into the skies once again, and I sat at the focal point within the High Cloud Court. To my left, my retinue took their seats in the pews of the first caste— my caste—the Storm Sorcerers. Lukos Thundergale, acting as my first advisor, sat in the front. Behind him, Solarynne, Azurynne, and Ohmyn populated the second row; Karynne, Imrythel, Yasmynne, and Nestryn the third. The Triad's clergy stood at the podium behind my chair; Atun's priest, Edamyn, at the center with Arlyn as Otarr's priest and Tasmynne as Selene's priestess at either of his sides. Silence hung over the court, and I watched the entourage of each caste gnoble filter into the room in ranking order—powdered and glittered Cloud Courtiers, darker complexioned Fire Forgers, small and deceptively peaceful-looking Frost Fighters, then the broad Stone Singers, and finally with dark glasses and their tentacled mustaches, the Underhill Dwellers. When each gnoble and their council had taken their respective seats from left to right in the semicircle, Edamyn called ascension to order.

His aged voice still strong, he invited the leaders, "Will each caste's gnoble state your name? Tasmynne Hallowgale of Selene will record your attendance for Nantai records."

I turned my head toward my retinue as Lukos stood and said, "I am Lukos Thundergale, acting first advisor to Lady Mairynne who is here before the Nantai people to accept the caste gifts and the treasures of the Nantai, and to take her oath."

As he sat, the foremost Cloud Courtier stood. "Lady Mairynne and Edamyn of Atun, in representation of the Cloud Courtiers, I am Gnoble Strato-Ymar." The courtier sat solemnly with a straight back and faced the next in line.

A dark-complexioned man stood. "Gnoble Yuos Atith of the Fire Forgers," he said efficiently and quickly dropped back into his seat.

A small woman in a silken cream-colored suit stood. When she spoke, her voice made music of the words. "Gnoble Lady Tenkara of the Frost Fighters."

Gruffly, the stocky but clearly feminine leader of the fifth caste said, "Gnoble Sarangarel, representing the Stone Singers." She smoothed a large necklace with many inlaid gems surrounding a blood-red ruby as she returned to her chair with a thunk.

Finally, the shorter man with long arms whom I'd met at midnight before lurched to his feet. He didn't remove the glasses shading his eyes, and his mustache twitched as he said, "Gnoble Brimr. Here from the

Northerly Barrows on behalf of the Underhill Dwellers."

"Welcome Gnobles of Nantai," Edamyn said as Brimr took his seat.

In the pause between his welcome and his next words, I considered the Tsinti and the Small Folk, mourning the fact that some peoples within Nantai lacked representation that day in the High Cloud Courts.

Edamyn didn't leave much room for consideration as he introduced himself, Amar, and Tasmynne, then called for the ceremony to continue. "Today, as the Nantai people bear witness, the Storm Sorcerer heir-selected, Mairynne Evangale, third daughter of Tennō Atheryn Evangale and Kōgō Noralynne, comes before you to receive the sacred treasures and swear her oath to the people. The days that follow begin the cleansing in preparation for the Daijō-sai in which she will commune with Otarr, seeking his blessing to take her place as empress of the Nantai people. Three days later, the festivals will follow. "Gnoble Strato-Ymar of the Cloud Courtiers shall present the first treasure."

The courtier Strato-Ymar seemed to drift in his long robes, with only small bends at the knees with each step toward me at the center of this affair. I caught myself wringing my hands and forcibly willed them still in my lap. The courtier reached the place where I sat and dropped to a kneel on the large pillow before me. The shoulder marking resembled a lily that grows in the valley near Stormskeep, assuring me I hadn't met this particular person.

"Lady Mairynne," Strato-Ymar began. "Upon Atun, the all-seeing God, Selene, the lady of the moon, bestowed a mirror that enabled him to see truth in all things. Atun's mirror remains encased in the temple of the Triad at Stormskeep's citadel. This mirror"—she held toward me an open box with a circular silver object resting on a black cushion—"is a replica of Atun's mirror, enchanted that you may see truth when you look upon the glass. May you use this justly as you take the seat of the Nantai people."

My mouth and throat parched, I ran my tongue over my teeth, hoping that the words I needed to voice would sound confident. I accepted the box. "I am honored, Strato-Ymar." Lifting the small object from its bed, I opened it and looked into the glass. My reflection stared back, my eyes worried. I turned the glass so it caught the reflection of the Cloud Courtier. She, yes, she looked softer in the glass, her face full and body shaped in nice curves; and in general, I found the softer image far more attractive than her homogenous and slender illusion. Smiling knowingly at her, I put away the mirror and accepted her hands. I echoed the words of Tennō Makenyn, "Humbly, I accept this treasure and pray to Atun for guidance in its use."

The trinket seemed like something that would be of use at the High Cloud Court, but it also felt like an invasion of these peoples' privacy. It was temptation, one that could be useful but could also hurt. For reasons I didn't understand, the Cloud Courtiers willfully changed their appearances into a look I assumed they considered collectively beautiful. That I disagreed mattered little. I vowed to myself that I would keep the mirror close but refrain from using it unless it seemed necessary to a matter of ruling my people.

Idly, I thought how my father had once endured this ceremony, receiving the same gifts as I accepted now. The stone resting against my chest burned as I wondered where his mirror had gone.

"Yuos Atith of the Fire Forgers," Edamyn said. "Please bring forth the sword."

The man came forward, scabbarded sword in hand.

He knelt onto both knees, head bowed, and held the sword with both hands across his thighs—one on the hilt and one on the sheath. He lifted eyes as black as coal to mine and said, "Mairynne Evangale, this sword carries no special enchantments. Yet my most talented Forgers wrought it from the purest ore vein in all of Nantai. In the same manner that Otarr, the Day-Seer, presented Atun, the All-Seer, with the heavenly Sword of Gathering Clouds, I present this to you, our empress. As Kōgō, may you see the clouds gathered for the nourishment of the Nantai people."

The lack of enchantment signified that the Storm Sorcerers, who could innately channel the clouds to water the crops, were indeed the Gods' intended ruling caste. Holding both hands forward to accept the second sacred treasure, I said, "I am honored, Yuos Atith." Once it rested in my palms, it felt light. I drew my brows together. "It seems smaller than the others." My father's sword, I recalled, stood almost to my shoulder when the tip rested on the ground. Likewise, when I had visited Otarr's sacred temple, all the retired swords had seemed larger than manageable. I slid the blade from its seat and appraised the blues and grays in the contours of the metal. This one I could hold easily at my side and would be able to swing with minor effort.

"Lady Mairynne, the Fire Forger priest crafted the blades from the blessed ore and under the watchful eyes of the Triad. Your blade is exactly as the Gods intended. I know not why it is so small." His brow furrowed in reflection of my own at his last words.

Reseating the sword and placing it on the ground next to Atun's mirror, I offered my hands to the Fire Forger. "Of course, Yuos Atith. I have faith that the blade is true. I humbly accept this treasure and pray to Atun for guidance in its usage."

When Yuos Atith had returned to his seat, Edamyn called forth Sarangarel of the Stone Singers to present the jewels. She brought forward a necklace with three gemstones. As she knelt on the pillow before me, she said, "This necklace represents the Triad itself and the gifts that Atun gave to Otarr and Selene in thanks for the mirror and the sword. The round black diamond at the center represents Atun himself. The yellow diamond on one side represents Otarr, and the silver half-moon on the other, Selene. May I, Kōgō Mairynne?" Sarangarel stood, her eyelashes fluttering as she waited for me to lean forward. When I did, she placed the necklace about my neck and turned to her people. Two of the broad men in her entourage brought forward a case and set it at my side. Without a word, Sarangarel flipped open the lid, flourishing her hands to present the jewels before sauntering back to her seat at the head of the Stone Singers.

The case full of twinkling jewels was the first of the caste gifts to their new empress. Afterward, each caste came forward in turn and offered gifts from their people. The Cloud Courtiers gave fine silks; the Fire Forgers brought fine household items of various metals; the Frost Fighters offered bottles and bottles of sweet wine; and the Underhill Dwellers offered scrolls of parchment for the royal library. As the gifts piled up around me, I worried, chewing the inside of my lip. Soon, it would be time for my oath.

When the gnobles had delivered the last packages, Edamyn's powerful voice called the group back to order. The murmurs died down and he said, "The giving of treasures and gifts is complete. It completes the first rite of Ascension. Now, Mairynne Evangale will take her oath to the people. Gnoble Brimr, bring forward the first of Kōgō Mairynne's annals."

I stood and turned as the gnoble lifted a heavy, ornately bound book and lumbered to the podium. He opened it to the first pages, opened the ink jar, and dropped in a sharpened feather. He held out his hands for me to take my position.

"Many thanks, Gnoble Brimr," Edamyn said.

As the Underhill Dwellers' gnoble returned to the rest of the Underhill Dwellers, I turned to Lukos and asked, "May I have the scroll?"

Silently, he delivered it unto my hands and returned to the seat at the head of the Storm Sorcerers. I spread it before me and carefully regarded each of the castes in attendance. At length, I said, "My people of Nantai, before I take my oath, I would read some words from the annals of Tennō Makenyn, the Scarred, first emperor of the Nantai people. As he prepared for his separation from the Kuroidragon, he wrote:

> The shamans say that this may well take my life. They say that if I am fortunate, I will live, but I will likely be unconscious for weeks, maybe longer. They say that even when I resurface from the depths of consciousness that I will be unfit to rule for many moons.
>
> I shan't wholly relinquish my right to rule the people. Before I undergo the extraction, my brother Morwyn shall take this oath and rule in my stead until I am once again able.

Lifting my eyes from the scroll, I scanned the faces in the semi-circular formation. Eyes were wide with shock, and the room didn't breathe or make a sound. They waited.

I went on, "Here, before the Storm Sorcerers, Fire Forgers, Frost Fighters, Stone Singers, and Underhill

Dwellers, I, Mairynne Evangale, third daughter and decreed heir of Tennō Atheryn, swear an oath to the Nantai people, and this is my oath."

Returning to the scroll and substituting names where necessary, I read:

> Until the return of our rightful emperor, Atheryn Evangale, I, Mairynne Evangale, shall rule the peoples of Nantai in his stead. I shall retain Tennō Atheryn's council. I shall honor the Triad and act as ruler in every way. I shall maintain annals that will be burned upon the return of our rightful ruler. Histories and laws that I record shall be nullified upon the return of Tennō Atheryn Evangale, but until that time, such histories and laws will remain in effect. Should Tennō Atheryn be unable to resume the Serpentine Throne, my annals will live on as if this oath were the enduring ruler's oath.

Gasps went up around the room, but I continued, now speaking the traditional words of the people. Raising my voice above the din, I said:

> Under Atun, the All-Seer, and under Otarr, the Day-Seer, I vow to honor the people of Nantai. I shall make the same vow to Selene, the Night-Seer, on this very night when she takes her place in the sky. I vow to see the people protected and fed. I give my oath to uphold the laws that have been laid within the annals before me, and I pledge to keep the traditions of the Nantai sacred. With the blessings of the Three Sacred Treasures, I accept ascension to the Serpentine Throne.

As I spoke, the people in the room had returned to a stunned silence, and as a result, I'd leveled out my volume by the time I finished and looked up from the scroll. Thirty, maybe more, wide eyes looked upon me.

It was done.

I was Kōgō Mairynne Evangale, empress of the Nantai people, if only for a time.

SEVEN

Sosano & Inara

THE PLUMPEST OF MY advisors waddled in a slow pace back and forth within the royal chambers, his hands shoved deep inside the pockets of his jerkin. Ohmyn Havengale, clearly more vexed than the others by the temporary nature of my oath, prattled on about how inappropriate the entire thing had been and how I should have discussed this with them beforehand. Karynne stood near a far wall, and each time I made eye contact during Ohmyn's monologue, she seemed to shrug in a manner that said she had advised as much. At my sister's side, Imrythel gave a few near imperceptible nods punctuating certain points voiced by the advisor. Her hard green stare and folded arms told me she firmly disagreed with my actions that day.

I pressed my fingers against my forehead and squeezed my eyes shut. My other advisors were also present and seated at the table in the royal common area. For a long time, not a one spoke in my favor or in my defense. I hadn't considered this moment, only the overwhelming drive inside me that told me this was the right path. Still, under such scrutiny, I held faith in the truth behind those feelings, and I waited for my advisors to work through their concerns.

Solarynne, at long last, interjected, "Ohmyn." Then she waited for him to stop and look at her.

Red-faced and eyes wide, he turned and snapped, "And now, you'll come out of your haze to join us?"

I made to stand, an objection on my tongue, but Solarynne held up a hand to forestall the chide I'd intended.

In her gaze, I could feel all the weight of a winter's storm and thanked the Triad she didn't focus her ire upon me. The temperature seemed to drop in the room as she said, "Havengale, you should be happy that your empress, Mairynne, has taken an oath that kept you as counselor. The fact that she spoke Morwyn's words leaves Tennō Atheryn's advisors in place by its very nature. Should she wish, she could write you off the council. So, I'd advise that you hold your tongue. She may be young, but she is your empress and your dissent borders on insubordination."

If possible, the red on Ohmyn's face deepened. "Does no one else object? Lukos? Azurynne?"

Lady Azurynne Nightingale shifted forward in her seat, but she portrayed little emotion as she said, "In this decision, what I believe matters little. I sit on this council to advise the ruler of the Nantai people based on our laws and what the Nightingale family holds ethical. Kōgō Mairynne's decision does not violate any values. That she has found a way to satisfy our demands but leave room for her father's return is acceptable in my eyes and the eyes of our written ways."

Ohmyn turned to his last hope for support.

Lukos shook his head. "There's wisdom in Lady Azurynne's words." After a pause, he added, "And in Lady Solarynne's."

I breathed a sigh, relieved that the majority of my council had accepted my oath, albeit reluctantly. However, my sigh had scarcely finished when the door flew open and Thalaj marched into the room.

Before he had even reached the table, he spouted, "What were you thinking, Mairynne?"

I popped out of my chair, regretting the words I would say, needed to say, before they gained voice. With my shoulders rolled back and chin lifted, I said, "Gensui Thalaj Northerngale, I have not requested your counsel in this matter. Nor have I requested your presence at my table. The royal council is no place for a guard. When we have completed our business here, I'll speak with you. Until then, you will wait in the outer room."

The few moments that followed seemed to stretch into eternity. Thalaj's face fell, then he gathered it into an impassive mask, pressed his lips tight, and pivoted to leave the room. All I could do was hope that he understood how I couldn't have such a conversation in front of my Storm Sorcerer counselors. Since I'd just barely gained the majority's support, I couldn't risk showing leniency toward the way that he'd blown into the room. I searched every face in the room, ensuring that I'd adequately retained my position. It seemed I had.

The last person I looked to was Karynne, and she offered a smile and a single nod. With that, the matter seemed well handled, and after our reconnection the night before, I felt thrilled to have her support once again.

Imrythel began, "Kōgō Mairynne, may I speak freely?" She ran a hand over the black lace covering her one eye.

Turning my gaze to her, I said, "Immediate family and their first advisors hold a place on the council. As my sister's first advisor, you are welcome to offer your thoughts on the matter." This, I offered as tradition, and custom dictated as much, though I had no desire to hear her concern.

"Very well," she started. "I will stop short of objecting to the vows you have sworn. But I fear that my people, the people of the Great Sands, may have issues with the nature of your oath. As I merely represent the Sandsgales, I feel it necessary to voice my concern."

Her words were smooth and showed the respect that Ohmyn Havengale's had not, so I motioned for her to continue.

"I would ask your leave to go to my people immediately and deliver this news in person. I believe their fear will drive continued unrest within the castes, but I'd like to confirm. If such an unrest were to escalate, it could lead to a struggle on many fronts. I think our biggest adversaries would be the Fire Forgers or the Frost Fighters, but I'd not count out the Cloud Courtiers either. Though they seem secure in their position of leading the High Cloud Court, would they pass on the opportunity to have a courtier rise to the station of emperor or empress?"

Lukos reached for a goblet and added to Imrythel's suggestions, "What she says also carries merit, Kōgō Mairynne."

Ohmyn flounced into a chair. Though tamed a bit, he added, "This unrest is what I'd warned of before. It is a danger that we should monitor heavily." Grabbing his empty goblet, he looked inside, then bellowed to the room, "Is there ale?"

From where I stood, I had line of sight to everyone in the room. I clasped my hands and said, "Imrythel, thank you for your counsel. I grant you leave. You'll return to Stormskeep to provide an update once you've delivered the news?"

"I will," she answered, tipping her head.

I continued, "None of the concerns are of consequence to the nature of my vows to the Nantai people now. I have sworn my oath, and we must now turn toward managing the people to avoid such uprisings."

"Might I make one suggestion, Kōgō Mairynne?" Imrythel asked.

"Of course."

"It might do you well to receive each of the gnobles and ask that they hold the impermanence of your vows in confidence," she said.

"That is sound advice," Lukos quickly and enthusiastically offered, "and it might go a long way in working to avoid a dethronement or attempts to usurp the Storm Sorcerers' hold on the highest caste, especially with the likes of the courtiers."

Karynne stepped forward. "I, for one, am proud of my sister. She showed a decisiveness that exists in few others. I believe she earned the throne today with her conviction and action. It will be smart to take measures to protect our station, but the result of the oath is the same. She is the Nantai empress, and she has authority to rule the people as she sees fit, and should our father not return, she will rule until her death when her successor takes her place."

Solarynne looked questioningly between Karynne and me, clearly surprised at my sister's sudden show of support. Had it not been for the midnight stroll, I would have had similar questions in my mind, but this was the Karynne I knew from before and the sister I was happy to have returned.

I spread my arms. "Counselors, you are all excused. Karynne, please stay. Imrythel, would you ask Thalaj to join us?"

∞∞∞∞∞∞∞∞∞∞∞∞

OBLIGING MY WISHES, EVERYONE departed; to which destinations, I didn't know. Nor did that concern me much. I went to my sister. "Thank you for supporting me."

"It would seem that your council is coming around. Ohmyn will be your greatest challenge. It will be a long time before he'll allow the matter to rest."

I pulled the pins that held my hair, allowing it to fall about my shoulders. "Do you know where over Nantai we are at this moment?"

"The last time I spoke with the navigators, we were traveling northwest over the Narrows toward the Copper Coast. Is there somewhere specific you're concerned about?"

"Nothing specific." My eyes drifted closed, and I breathed deeply, expanding my lungs to allow the air to refresh my body. The Narrows was a strait far to the south. I'd been attempting to keep track of the route since our arrival and found it strange that I could only vaguely sense the quick-paced travel while on the cloud island. Sometime tomorrow, we'd pass the Copper Coast and be near the Evernight Marshes.

The door opened, drawing me out of my calculations. I opened my eyes just as Imrythel entered. My sister's advisor went to her side and whispered in her ear. Thalaj, on her trail, stopped just inside the room. My first guard stood with his feet at shoulder width, hands clasped behind his back, and his look betrayed no thought or feeling. Knowing I'd taken him down before, all I had now was hope that he'd see the reason behind my words and understand, or at least trust, that my scold had been necessary.

At a side table, I refilled my goblet with a sweet sparkling wine. "I begin to wonder if this day will ever end," I said to the room, but looking at no one. "Though when Otarr retires for the evening, the Hallowgales require my presence at the Cloud Temple to begin a cleansing process only known to the Gods and the clergy who represent them. Why don't we know more about what that entails?"

Silence hovered in response to my question. At length, Imrythel answered, "Kōgō Mairynne, it is a sacred rite. Outside of the people who complete the rite, only those trained as a Hallowgale are privileged enough in the eyes of the Triad to hold that knowledge."

She'd said the obvious, what everyone had learned as younglings, but it didn't allay my exhaustion at these formalities. "Well, I'd rather not go through these rites, and I don't relish the thought of the celebrations to follow." I gazed through the windows. Many hours remained before this would all begin, and I needed a distraction. "Tell me more about the search party and the plans to find Father."

"Mairynne," started Karynne, "we've already told you the extent—"

"May I?" Imrythel interrupted, placing a hand on my sister's shoulder. When Karynne nodded, her advisor continued, "Thalaj can convey anything you wish to know about that topic. And, given the tension before, I think it would be good for the two of you to talk. I would like to prepare for my journey to the Great Sands, and I'd like to confer with Karynne before my departure."

I folded my brow in confusion. "If we are truly over the Narrows, we are many leagues from your home. Wouldn't it be easier and quicker to wait for the High Cloud Court to make the full evolution? Then you'd be able to simply descend on a gale rather than having to travel overland."

"If the route of the cloud island were due north, that would be true, Kōgō Mairynne. However, the plan is to travel north along the western coast of Nantai, then across the Iced Plains. By morning, we'll be passing over the Copper Coast, and it would be quicker to travel overland from there to my home."

"Imrythel," Karynne said, "I'd rather not attend the celebrations while you leave. Maybe I should go with you."

The two exchanged looks, some unheard conversation carried on within their shared gaze. Instead of answering directly, Imrythel said, "I think you should be here for your sister, but we can discuss it further. Should we go?"

Thalaj didn't move a muscle during this exchange.

Karynne turned to me. "Do you have further need of me today?"

"No," I answered. "You may go. Thank you again for supporting me with the counselors." Before they turned to go, I caught a green flash in Imrythel's eye as she moved her gaze between my sister and me.

Alone with Thalaj, I said, "Please, be at ease." I motioned to the wine and took a seat.

Stiffly, Thalaj remained where he stood. "You requested my presence. What might I do for you, Kōgō?"

Though I regretted my necessary harshness before, I used it once again. "You may grab a glass of wine, water if you prefer, then sit with me and have a conversation." Softer, I added, "I don't wish to command you, Thalaj. It's just the two of us now. Can't we just talk?"

He relented, poured himself a goblet from the water pitcher, and sat across the table from the chair I'd taken.

Formal expectations hovered in the air, and he would wait hours for me to break the silence.

Sighing, I began, "Before, my response to your demands emphasized our caste difference." I ran two fingers up and down the fat stem of the goblet, stroking the ridges of the pottery as I continued, "Unfortunately, in this room, with my father's counselors, I had too much at stake to allow you to question my motives too." I paused, waiting for him to answer.

His words came stiffly. "Mairynne, I meant no disrespect, but I need to know why you took such an oath. This is one of my duties to the throne"—he hesitated— "but it also comes from my concern for you."

Leaning forward, I extended a hand to him but couldn't quite reach. To my relief, he met me partway, placing his hand in mine.

"Thalaj," I said. "I welcome you to speak to me openly when we are alone. However, I can't afford to have anyone question your position in relation to their own. As Father taught me well, this is an unfortunate and necessary approach as ruler of the Nantai people. By our very nature, we position ourselves toward a higher caste, always seeking ways to gain the next level within our individual hierarchies." I ducked my head to secure eye contact. "You are not like that, and I also believe differently. But Father always said that without that order, the Nantai people would become lost."

"Then I truly don't understand why you took a temporary oath."

At that, I stalled, took a drink of the sweet wine, looked around the room, then met his dark eyes forcefully. Quietly, but with emphasis, I said, "I told you before that I intend to search for my father at your side."

"No, Mairynne. You can't go. Once you commune with Otarr and Selene, you must remain in Stormskeep to rule the people. This ensures the order so told to you by Tennō Atheryn."

"Thalaj, yes. I can. And I will." I sighed. "You can leave this part to me. In fact, I want to go to Umbra with you. I feel that the people would be more amicable to parting with their relic if I were to offer some diplomatic terms. They are, after all, Nantai people too."

Thalaj shifted in his seat, straightened his spine, and inhaled sharply, an obvious objection working its way up his throat and struggling to gain voice.

Holding up an index finger, I continued, "But I understand that this is impossible right now. Such diplomacy will have to wait."

He relaxed if only by a small measure.

I continued, "But I think you should leave the courts and begin your journey into the Evernight Marshes while I tend to these cleansing rites and preside over the celebrations to follow."

"How can I ensure your safety here while I'm gone?"

"You brought a team. I've been in no genuine danger here. Do you not trust your selected people to see me guarded?"

"I trust the people I brought beyond doubt, but—"

I interrupted, "There are too many people with eyes on me here. I will be fine. And I'd like you to return to Stormskeep as soon as possible so we can understand how we can use this token from Umbra to find the Tsinti and figure out what happened to my father. This waiting and politicking is eating me alive."

Thalaj remained quiet, but his throat worked as if he swallowed what he wanted to say.

"Tomorrow, we should be passing through the skies somewhere over the Copper Coast. That is not far from the Evernight Marshes. You should go then. Do you need help in calling a gale strong enough to lower you safely to the surface?"

"Most likely." Thalaj lowered his eyes. "As only half Storm Sorcerer, my storm magic is not as strong as yours or others, and the air is thinner up here."

I'd assumed as much and said, "You brought Roryn with you on this detail. Since you were going to take him on the journey, maybe you should take him tomorrow. I'll probably be in a bath somewhere in the temple—being useless." I huffed and reclined in my chair.

"Mairynne, that only leaves you with two guards."

I gave him a hard stare. It worked to stop his objection, but he returned it with his dark eyes.

In this silent exchange, a screech pealed through the space beneath the cloud island, shaking the very foundation of the royal chambers. Standing, I rushed to the door and out onto the balcony. As I was closer to the door, I reached the edge before my first guard, but Thalaj came quickly to my side. Beyond the railing and far below, the southernmost part of Nantai appeared as a narrow strip of land between two expansive blue seas— the Syrensea to the west and the Mannakasea to the east.

"What was that?" I asked, my pulse thudding hard in my throat. "The same we heard at the Falls?"

Thalaj shook his head gravely, pushing in front of me protectively. "I wish I had an answer," he said, his eyes growing darker than usual, seeming concerned as he turned and ushered me back inside. "But it definitely sounds like something you shouldn't face until we know more."

I pushed against him, struggling to see something over the balcony, anything that may have caused the ear-splitting noise. He wielded his lithe strength gently, but it was more than a match for me, and I soon found myself back inside and behind the glass. When he had secured the door, he turned and said, "I never discovered its source after that night by Stormskeep Falls."

Before we could further discuss, counselors from every corner of the royal chambers moved quickly, steps fueled by fear, into the room. Everyone asked after the sound at once, and though I trembled with the same fear, I had the burden of addressing my people—even my leaders. I turned and moved deeper into the room, holding both hands high. "Counselors, please . . ." I started.

Karynne placed her fingers in the corners of her mouth and whistled. When everyone looked at her, she motioned to me.

"Thank you, Sister."

She dipped her head.

"We mustn't panic. Certainly, a bird of prey is hunting this night, and the sound is different here. There is naught for us to fear inside."

Ohmyn shook his head, his cheeks blubbering. "That was no bird. There was the same sound over Stormskeep a fortnight past."

Karynne cleared her throat and calmly moved to my side. "Kōgō Mairynne speaks the truth. That sound is but a screech owl. It has been many years, but I heard it during my travels with Mother and Father."

I smiled my thanks to her, not putting much faith in the explanation but needing everyone to remain calm. "Return to your evening routines. All is well."

As directed, they shuffled back into their individual rooms, murmuring all the while.

◇◇◇◇◇◇◇◇◇◇◇◇◇◇◇◇

TASMYNNE, PRIESTESS OF SELENE, had woven my hair into uncounted braids upon completion of the cleansing rituals; and my scalp felt drawn, the corners of my eyes slanted, my brows and forehead pulled taut. The acolytes assured me the tension would ease after a few days, a matter I felt grateful for as I'd wear them for a full cycle of the moon goddess as tradition prescribed.

"When Selene's full face shines over Nantai once again, you may release these bonds," Tasmynne had said as she finished the work.

My scalp throbbed as I sat on the dais in the high court room turned celebration hall; I leaned to my left and whispered to Karynne, "Did Thalaj leave while I was at the temple?"

"He did along with his guard, Roryn. On what mission did you send them?"

I shook my head. "Nothing of importance. He should be at Stormskeep by the time we return."

My sister gazed upon me as if she wanted to question my motives further but decided to either trust my judgment or simply allow it to rest. Instead, she said with a smile, "The braids are a lovely look for you, Mairynne."

"You jest, Karynne." I laughed off her praise.

"No, I speak only in truth."

Under the dimly lit orbs floating near the ceiling, the gnobles and their retinues each wandered leisurely into the hall, gathering in small clusters and holding individual conversations. I envied their seemingly carefree vitality now that the time for formality had passed. We were there to celebrate the Nantai people ushering in a new era. Every caste wore their finest attire, and despite the veritable rainbow of colors, each set of tunics, dresses, or robes gleamed under orb-light. The very attire my people wore bespoke a lightness in the air. Yet somehow, I couldn't join my people in their frivolity.

Lifting a hand to the back of my head, I said, "If only they felt so lovely." I gave a small, sad laugh and dropped my hand. Karynne and I both looked around the room, holding a silent conversation. It seemed that everyone present had someone, and that night we drifted together as the only two who missed another half. I made another effort to extend our banter, "Imrythel departed for the Great Sands?"

Karynne nodded. On my other side and in her typical fashion, Yasmynne cuddled up to Nestryn and engaged little with others, but they seemed enthralled by the gathering of all the castes around the center stage. The scene that awaited looked like a living mountain top where a river sprang forth. Boulders and green grasses surrounded the spring. I'd never seen the legend of Sosano and Inara enacted by the Cloud Courtiers, but I marveled already at the illusions built into the set—a gently swaying tree, ever-running water, and blades of grass moving as if a wind swept through the room.

A fine meal, a feast in truth, lay before me. Although, after two nights and two days of fasting, I had communed with the Gods just before being led into the celebration hall. My appetite well sated with the sweet wine and sacred grains of the Gods, I couldn't bring myself to partake. Gnobles came forward at regular intervals to pay their respect and make conversation easily forgotten. String musicians on a balcony serenaded the guests as they finished their dinner and moved closer toward the hall's center for better views of the upcoming performance.

I sipped warmed ruby wine and observed my people for what seemed an eternity, until they stopped arriving, stopped eating, and the din of conversation almost overshadowed the music. As I sat there, fighting exhaustion, the door opened and a herald entered, motioning to the percussionist who stood on a pedestal near the door. The courtier on the percussion stand, guised to be larger than the others and dressed only in simple *ketill* pants, nodded. He lifted a mallet and struck the bell.

One . . . two . . . a dozen times, and the people encircled the stage, falling into silent anticipation. At all grand Nantai celebrations, the hosts arranged for the enactment of the most famous Nantai legend, "The Spirit Sosano, the Blooming Princess, and the Regalia of the Nantai." I had seen it a dozen or more times that I could recall, only once with a single Cloud Courtier amidst the troupe, but never with the combined talents of the illusionists.

The orbs around the room dimmed as a narrator in long black robes and a black-feathered mask moved around the stage, flourished arms toward the crowd, and sent glittering sparks to encircle the set. The sparks lifted to the heavens, revealing three people huddled on the mountain top near the head of the River Hi. An old man comforted his wife, and a woman in the prime of her beauty stood brave-faced in a simple sheath dress, wearing a string of bright, tooth-shaped jewels.

As the narrator began, I found myself leaning forward and taking note of every minor element. The scene itself familiar, the details enabled by illusionary magic painted a more original experience than I could ever recall. When the old man cried, his tears glittered like diamonds trailing slowly down his cheek. When the old woman wailed, my chair shook with her sorrow.

The black-robed narrator, double-timbred and harmonious, continued, ". . . and Sosano, Spirit of the Storm, descended from the heavens above and went to the Father. He asked the old man why he cried so, and the old man replied, 'The eight-forked serpent will soon come to devour our last daughter, Inara.' "

The old woman wailed, and I felt her pain as my own. The actors mutely portrayed their characters before the Nantai gnobles, and the crowd was as enraptured as I. The black-robed narrator danced around the mountain top, driving the legend forward: "Sosano replied, 'If you will give me thy daughter, I will save her from the serpent, slay him, and honor your daughter for eternity.'

"And so the old man and the old woman kneeled at the spirit's feet and begged for Sosano to make it so, for their daughter to live. Thus Sosano took their daughter. With the magic of the storms, he called forth a great spinning wind that encircled Inara, and when it left, a blooming tree stood in her place beside the headwaters of the River Hi.

"Then Sosano bade the old man and woman brew eight tubs of sweet wine and place them in larger tubs of bitter-milk spirits. He instructed the man and woman to place them in a circle around the tree of the Blooming Spirit and to hide in the surrounding trees and await the arrival of the eight-headed serpent."

My hand idly drifted to cover my mouth. Where before, this had all been mythos in my mind, I then connected the story with the cleansing ritual I'd just experienced. A rite in which I ceremoniously drank from eight goblets and bathed in bitter-milk baths. A pairing with this story bloomed in my chest that hadn't existed before, and I watched and listened with every fiber of my soul while the next scene unfolded.

"When the serpent came, eight sets of eyes glowed like the red of winter's cherry, and on its back, firs and cypresses grew. But when it slithered to the headwaters of the River Hi, the sweet wine and bitter milk distracted the heads. Each head drank deeply and sank into drunken sleep.

"Whilst the serpent slept, Sosano drew his ten-span sword and chopped the serpent into pieces. When he split the serpent's belly, he found the Eight-Span Mirror of Truth and laid it at the base of the Blooming Spirit that was Inara and continued about his work.

"When he came to the tail, the blade rang and came away notched. Sosano dissected the tail to reveal a bright sword. He washed it in the River Hi and held it to the heavens. When he did this, clouds gathered above, opening with cleansing rain. The rain washed away the blood from the grasses and dissolved the serpent to fertilize the ground. Green, wet grass shone with small diamonds on each blade where Sosano had slain the serpent. And he named the blade the Sword of Gathering Clouds.

"When the serpent had gone and the rain had cleared, Sosano took the Sword of Gathering Clouds to the Blooming Spirit and turned her back into the woman, Inara. Thankful that he'd saved her from her sisters' fates, she bestowed the tooth-shaped jewels upon him. Sosano made Inara his wife in the early morning when Otarr and Selene both gazed over the land. After they had married, he presented his gifts of thanks to the Gods. To Otarr, he gave the Sword of Gathering Clouds. To Selene, the Eight-Span Mirror of Truth. And to Atun, he presented the jewels.

"And so the Nantai Treasures came to be and the Spirit of the Storm, Sosano, lived eternally at the headwaters of the River hi with his wife, Inara, the Blooming Spirit."

The scene at the center of the room fell into darkness and the orbs illuminated the awestruck audience. When the center came back into the light, the actors and set alike had vanished. Gasps went up around the room. Silently and still, I remained. I'd never known how closely the legend of Sosano and Inara was linked to the emperor's or empress's regalia and our rituals, and I felt simultaneously proud to be Nantai empress and heavy in the chest. Whether it had been the illusionary talents of the Cloud Courtiers or the reality of my ascension and cleansing, I couldn't be certain, but this enactment of the well-known legend rang so poignantly that a tear leaked from one eye as the actors returned and bowed to the audience.

The percussionist's mallet struck a shield, sending a long singular ring through the room and marking the end.

Applause erupted.

The black-robed narrator came and bowed low at my feet, the feathers of his mask brushing along my skirts. Silently then, the courtier stood and looked me in the eyes, the gray of his irises and the surrounding glittering white set into a coal-black skin within the even blacker mask setting me on edge. A chill ran from my neck to my tailbone as the narrator turned away and retreated.

I longed for Thalaj.

EIGHT

A Spellcaster in Arashi

GRAY CLOUDS HAD OVERCAST Arashi on the day we'd embarked upon the High Cloud Court, hiding the color of our land from sight. That wasn't so when the misted island returned to Stormskeep. As we, the Storm Sorcerers, had been the first to climb those misty stairs, we would also be the first to disembark. As the island began its descent under Otarr's heat, the falls at Stormskeep appeared small in the distance. But as the cloud foundation descended further and encircled the keep's highest spire, they grew larger, pouring between lush greenery from the cliff.

It put me in mind of the Sosano reenactment.

At my side, Karynne sighed, her shoulders dropping with the long sound of relief. "It feels good to see our home again. I am certain it will feel even better to rest in my own bed this night."

The entirety of the High Cloud Court of Gnobles stood in a semicircle to bid my party farewell. In my time at the High Cloud Court, I had learned an impressive many things about the Nantai people. My people. Yet mystery and curiosity had loomed around every corner. After Yasmynne's assignation at Tsanseri's court, I hadn't seen Alto-Trea again, but Tsanseri herself had come to the royal chambers the morning after the celebrations to offer me her well wishes. She had looked humble, unlike how she'd presented herself at court, and offered me a cuff.

She instructed that I should wear it against the skin on my upper right arm at all times. "'Tis but a pretty bauble, Kōgō, but it may be of use one day," she added before kissing me on both palms, then either cheek, and finally taking her leave.

It'd been an unexpected gesture, but in the end, it reassured me to have her favor.

There on the cloud deck, I locked eyes with Tsanseri before I took the first misty step toward my castle's roof. We'd each dispensed with the familiarity, reassuming our regal personas. I touched the cuff beneath my sleeve, and she gave an almost imperceptible nod.

Down I went, anxious to be home, to see my aunt, to see how Corwyn had recovered, and to see Thalaj. He should have returned by now, and I grasped onto the notion I'd soon be off onto my own adventure in search of my father. Like many times before, the thought of Father heated the stone around my neck.

Both feet planted atop Stormskeep's high tower, I moved forward to allow the others room and scanned the roof. A sole acolyte, apprentice to the priest Arlyn of Otarr, awaited our arrival. The boy, unknown to me, watched and waited with more aplomb than I would expect of one so young. His parents had likely dedicated him to the Triad's service at birth. Arlyn gusted past me, wind shifting my skirt, and went to the acolyte. They stood close; the boy, while possessing a youth's wiry build, stood eye-to-eye with the priest. I couldn't hear their conversation, but from the quick words, there seemed urgency in his message. After a moment, Arlyn turned, a shadow across his face.

Unconscious of my steps, I joined them. "What is the trouble?"

Arlyn bowed his head. "Kōgō Mairynne, Nadialynne Riversgale requires your presence at the House of Healing."

"Still?" I demanded, looking between the priest and his apprentice. "Corwyn is still not well? Do we know what happened? Or from what he suffers?"

Arlyn shook his head and opened his mouth to speak, but it was the boy who answered first.

"Kōgō," he said, his head bowed and waiting.

It was the first time I'd met a subject beyond my household, my council, and the attendants to the High Cloud Court. I gaped at him, not wishing to accept the title for the heavenly sovereign. It took me a long moment to realize that he awaited my permission. Blinking, I shook off my surprise and said, "Please, continue."

The boy looked up, his bright eyes easily holding my gaze. He'd shown the proper respect and my royal position hadn't intimidated him, further clarifying that he'd been preparing for his position amongst our clergy for many moons. "The healers are not sharing what happened, but Lady Nadia asked me to await your return inside the spire. She bade that I fetch you to the House of Healing without delay."

"Lead the way." I held a hand forward to the acolyte, then motioned to the two guards that Thalaj had assigned for my protection.

They, along with Karynne, joined us. Instead of going to the stairs and descending through the keep, we went to the roof's edge. Arlyn called an updraft and held it steady while the other five stepped into the air. I grasped my skirt tight about my legs and joined them. As Arlyn eased the flow of magic, we floated downward until our feet touched the soft grass at the base of the castle's stone walls.

Arlyn then stumbled, leaned against the stone, and said between heavy breaths, "Too much magic. You have enough help." He looked at each of the guards. "I'm going to retire and recover."

I reached for him. "You should have asked us to help with the magic."

Arlyn waved me off. "I'll be well, Kōgō. Please go; tend to your family. Baldwyn?"

To his senior priest, Baldwyn said, "I shall return to you in your chambers shortly." Then to us, he added, "This way." He turned for the city street and onward toward the House of Healing.

Karynne at my side, we followed. I told my sister what little information I had, which felt like significantly less than I should know. When we arrived, we continued through the clean and sparsely furnished front rooms to a door at the end of a long hall. Inside, Corwyn sat upright in the bed, pale with ashen circles beneath both eyes, and he'd lost enough weight that his shoulder and arm bones made him look more square than normal. Nadia sat at the bedside, holding his hand. She had tired shadows under her eyes, but otherwise appeared well. She kissed her consort's cheek, came around the foot of his bed, and opened her arms for a hug.

Although I imagined I lent her my strength, as we embraced, she asked, "How are you, Mairynne?"

I gave a mirthless laugh. "How am I? You've been here worrying over Corwyn's health since we left, and you're asking how I am?"

Serenely, Nadia smiled, shifting her eyes over to Karynne then back to mine. "I believe Sentei Summergale is waiting. Would you join me in speaking with the healer?"

"Of course."

Nadia turned to my sister. "Karynne, will you remain with Corwyn? If he has any major tremors, call down the hall for us."

We all looked at the frail man in the bed who, as if to demonstrate the tremors, lifted a shaky cup to his mouth and sipped. Nadia took my arm, and we left the room.

My aunt tapped on the door across the hall, cracked it open, and said, "Sentei?"

Rustling came from within, and the healer said, "Come. Do come in, Lady Nadia." His voice, though gentle, sounded as if it echoed around the bottom of a metal jug, and when the door widened, a small, balding man with a thin nose stood in the opening. Exacerbating his birdlike appearance, his eyes and mouth both gaped as he gained sight of me. He bowed. "Kōgō."

I ground my teeth and closed my eyes for a second as I grappled with accepting the new formality. Releasing a sigh and settling my gaze back onto the healer, I said, "Sentei Summergale, please be at ease."

He, well-seasoned in his profession, accepted his

title far better than I accepted being formally addressed as the ruler by my people. It reinforced how ill-prepared I remained for this duty. I preferred to hear my name, or even Lady Mairynne, over Kōgō, the title for the heavenly sovereign. That my family still used my given name was a small blessing. I couldn't bear the burden of losing my identity in entirety.

The healer and Nadia shared a knowing look, and the birdlike man waved a hand toward a small table and chairs in the far corner of the room beneath the only window. "Do have a seat and let us discuss Corwyn's condition."

I went toward the offered seat, scanning the shelves that lined the long room. Someone had aligned corked bottles with various liquids, powders, and dried leaves or petals in meticulous rows. Each had a neatly scribed label, but I only recognized a few names—among them daisai, which I'd taken before to relieve the cramping around my cycle, and umeboshi which calmed a turning stomach. On the table, a book, larger than the annals I'd spent days pouring over in the royal library, sat open and scrolls littered the shelves behind where the healer had obviously been reading.

Silently, Nadia went to the window and gazed into the gardens where the healer apprentices tended to numerous herbs and flowers. I stood across the table, waiting, and Sentei scurried to the book.

"Look." The healer paused and pointed. "Do read here," he said, indicating some small script about halfway down the page.

I looked down to where he pointed and read aloud, "Primlock. Grows on the Lower Peninsula of Yōtei. If consumed will cause vomiting, diarrhea, tremors, sores in the mouth, difficulty breathing, and convulsions often resulting in death." I jerked my gaze up from the page, searching between the healer and my aunt. Nadia gave a tight-lipped nod with eyes that told me I understood correctly before I even asked the question. Heedless of that assurance, my question spilled out, "Are you stating that someone has poisoned Corwyn?"

"Yes. You have my meaning." The healer wrung his hands.

"Who would do such a thing to such a harmless man? Corwyn never so much as raises his voice." Again, I looked between Sentei Summergale and Nadia.

They exchanged another look.

"What?" I demanded.

Nadia sighed. "Have a seat, Mairynne." She took the chair across the table and the wiry healer sat as well. "I believe someone tried to poison me, not Corwyn."

I didn't want to sit; so tentatively and ready to stand again, I lowered myself to the very edge of the chair. First they'd informed me that someone who lived within my household suffered from poison derived from a plant not existing near Arashi, and to add to the matter, the poisoner had possibly intended to target another within my family. Hadn't we been through enough? What if the intended target hadn't been Nadia? I bit my lip, hard enough to feel piercing pain, but just shy of drawing blood. Forcing my voice to remain level, I asked, "How can you be so sure it's this"—I looked back at the page to recall the word—"primlock?" Beside the word was a sketch of a fluted red flower. Beneath the description of the effects, the underlined word *antidote* sat lonely on the page, nothing listed in the blank space.

"All." Sentei Summergale paused again after the single word answer, a manner in his speech I found quite odd. "Corwyn Dawnsgale has had all the symptoms listed. I've searched this book and the remainder of my library." He motioned to a tall shelf in a recess behind me I hadn't noticed. Books towered from floor to ceiling. My heart continued to fall as I turned back to him. He pointed a bony finger to the page. "This. This is the only ailment that lists every indicator. And though the book also states it often causes immediate death, those who survive display every single symptom that Corwyn has experienced."

My voice felt hollow as I asked the next logical, yet fruitless question, "Will he survive?"

Nadia sat in silence, her lip quivering and tears brimming in her eyes.

"Hope." The healer took her hand. "All we can do right now is hope he will recover. I am watching him closely and treating the symptoms, but I've never treated primlock poisoning."

"And it says immediate death is more frequent," I mused, considering how Jessa had suddenly turned up dead not so very long before Corwyn fell ill. I stood, faced the window, and ran my sweaty palms over my skirts. "Who would do this thing?" The question seemed empty, and certainly neither Nadia nor Sentei Summergale had the answer. Indeed, I hadn't expected one.

"Something." Sentei Summergale's face twisted. "There is something else. A symptom you should now about, Kōgō. In the nailbeds at the tips of Corwyn Dawnsgale's fingers, there is a discoloration. A greenish tent. Take a look when you return." The man looked down and wrung his hands. "It was the same for Jessamynne Feathergale."

I froze. Inside the healer's workshop and library,

the air thickened and grew even more stale, no wind to speak of, a great contrast to the gardens just beyond the window's panes. At length, I pulled my gaze away from the fertility outside. To my aunt, I asked, "What have you done to protect yourself and Corwyn from another poisoning?"

Nadia looked down, then uncertainly back up. Running a finger along a groove in the table, she said, "Everything we consume, I prepare by my own hand, or Sentei Summergale administers."

Inconvenient, but a necessity. "Very well. We will have to figure out a way to further protect you while we try to discover the source of the poisoning. Where is Thalaj? Has he returned?"

Nadia's brows knit. "We thought he traveled with you."

"No, he left the High Cloud Court on an errand. I thought he'd have returned by now."

"Kōgō," the healer started.

I flipped a hand to indicate he should continue.

"Careful," he said. "Do take caution with whom you share this information. And do consider protecting yourself, as well as your house, until we find who is responsible."

I glared at him. The accusation—mild though it may have been—stirred ire within. "If there is one person I trust implicitly, Sentei, it is Gensui Thalaj Northerngale. I just need him to return to set the investigation into motion. In the meantime, do you have other ideas on how we can protect my family and those who attend to us?"

"A taster. A poison taster, Kōgō?"

"I couldn't condemn anyone else to such a fate. What

kind of ruler would that make me? Does the primlock have any detectable smell or other property?"

"Unknown. The information I have given is all that I possess. But . . ." He scratched his beak-like nose.

"Yes? But what?" I prompted.

"Golems. There is a woman in the Bottomside district who practices the Small Folk's magic. Castings on stones and the like. She brews many of my potions, but she has some rumored skills in animation that we might find useful."

My eyes widened on an inhale. "A single-purpose golem taster for each of us. Perfect. Send someone to have her complete the task." When Sentei Summergale nodded, I turned to Nadia. "Do you have any thoughts on why someone would want to poison you?"

"I have two. It's either linked with your mother's murder—"

"Do we know if she suffered the same fate?" I interrupted.

Nadia shook her head.

"Inconclusive," said Sentei Summergale. "We can't be certain. I checked my notes for when we examined the empress's body, but I made no note of the green fingertips. It is possible I missed it."

I expelled a breath, my shoulders sagging. "That would have been too easy of an explanation, especially given the fact that Father went missing rather than turned up dead. What was your second thought, Nadia?"

She remained utterly still. "Someone may have discovered that you would name me as your first advisor."

That didn't seem possible. "We were alone in my

chambers when I asked that of you, and I had told no one at the time Corwyn fell ill. Did you share with anyone else?"

She gave a slight head shake. "No one but Corwyn himself."

"Very well. The—"

The door flew open, and an apprentice healer appeared panting. When he caught sight of me, he straightened and tried to gain his breath. He addressed me formally, "Kōgō," and bowed his head, his chest still heaving with exertion.

"Go ahead," I snapped.

"Sentei, we need you to attend to another patient. He's badly battered."

"Pardon." He stood and shuffled to the door. "Excuse me, Kōgō and Lady Nadia," he mumbled as he shuffled toward the door.

Nadia and I exchanged a questioning look. I hesitated, then curious I followed Sentei Summergale, my aunt in my wake. In the front of the House of Healing, I sighted a familiar face, a guard, Roryn—Thalaj's travel companion—pulling a litter.

My hand over my mouth, I ran to the man crumpled on the litter.

◇◇◇◇◇◇◇◇◇◇◇◇◇◇◇

SENTEI SUMMERGALE SHOUTED ORDERS to Roryn and the apprentice healers to carry Thalaj to another room and place him on a table at waist height. I refused to leave his side. I'd sent him to this fate, so they would have to work around me.

"Thalaj," I whispered over and over again close to

163

his battered face, hoping he'd hear and it might help that I was there with him.

His only replies were grunts, moans, and a long mewl as they stretched his body long for a more thorough examination. However, he held his hands constantly in tight fists, white about the knuckles.

When Roryn had arrived, dragging him into the House of Healing, he'd barely been holding on to consciousness. During the examination, he opened his eyes only once, and when he saw me, he grabbed my hand with more strength than I would have imagined he could possibly have possessed. He placed a small object in my hand, hissed in sudden pain, and drifted into oblivion.

Though I could see with my eyes how he suffered from physical abuse rather than poison, I still needed more proof. I turned his hands to look at the coloring around his fingernails. Dirt- and blood-crusted, but no hint of green. The healers cleaned, bandaged, and examined Thalaj thoroughly, an easier task after he succumbed to his body's need for rest. With the blood scrubbed away, I examined his hand again. Only the normal olive color of his skin stared back at me. I sagged with relief.

Sentei Summergale dripped some liquid into the side of his mouth. "Sleep," the healer said. "The potion will keep him asleep as my students tend to his wounds. It appears he has been on the losing end of a combat, but no concerns similar to my other patient." He and the apprentices worked around me for some time more.

I watched Thalaj swallow reflexively. He rested and I sat by his head, watching and waiting, my fingers itching to touch his bruised eye or split lip. But I resisted the temptation and wrung my hands in my lap.

Sentei Summergale had departed, leaving us with

two of his healer apprentices to finish the work.

A young woman laid a hand on my shoulder. "Kōgō?"

I looked away from the blossoming bruise on my first guard's chin. "Yes?" Sensing her hesitation and fearing the worst, I rushed to ask, "What is it?"

"You may not want to remain for this part. Setting bones makes an awful sound, one that most people never wish to hear."

By the door, Roryn blanched, turned, and left the room.

"No. I will stay." I swallowed, turning my gaze to Thalaj, then back to the woman. "The fault for his condition is mine, and I will bear witness to his recovery."

She nodded and positioned herself on the other side of the table at Thalaj's hip. She held his upper leg while another apprentice—a visibly stronger apprentice—grabbed onto his ankle and pulled, twisting slightly. The girl had spoken truth in her warning. Like the repeated sound of a whip or dozens of whips, the bone crackled and snapped as it searched for its natural position. The apprentice pulling grunted, furrowing his brow and setting his mouth in a tight line. From his apparent frustration, it seemed the bones might remain misaligned. He relented briefly, studying the shape of Thalaj's other leg, then adjusted his stance and went at it again. This time, chills raced up and down my arms as the sound of eggshells underfoot echoed around the room. At last, Thalaj's leg emitted a thunk, and the apprentice sagged over his work, sweat beading on his forehead.

He sighed as he caught my questioning stare and offered a quick nod. I eased a bit, happy that the sound was over, but also reassured that he'd gotten the bone back into place. Carefully, they wrapped the broken leg in linen, prepared a thick paste, and smeared it over the linen. This, they did several more times, then placed the casted leg on a pillow.

When their remaining bandaging and other ministrations were complete, they wheeled the table down the hall toward Corwyn's room but turned into one of the closer doors. I followed, still refusing to leave him alone. They moved Thalaj to a bed and covered him with a fresh blanket. When he was well settled, Sentei Summergale came to me and rested a hand on my arm. "Kōgō," he said and waited.

I nodded to give him leave to speak, tears brimming in my eyes and a lump in my throat preventing my words.

"He will rest for many hours now. You may return to your family. We will care for him well."

Scrubbing away the tears, I gave him a hard stare. "No. As I told your apprentice, I will remain with him."

The healer gave a semblance of a smile and said gently, "I understand," and left the room. I believed that he did understand my pain as I watched him go. Clearly, he had years of experience with this manner. Alone with my guard, I pulled up a chair and sat between Thalaj and the window. How long I remained there, I couldn't say.

Nadia came sometime later. "Mairynne," she said, sinking to her knees at my side.

My tears flowed again. They'd streaked my cheeks before, but I hadn't noticed. Now they rewet the crusty trails.

Soothingly, my aunt said, "This is not your fault."

"Nadia, I sent him into this."

Her eyes held only compassion as I looked into their depths for answers. She replied with a demanding question, "Do you think for one moment that this man went unwillingly at your behest?"

I bit my bottom lip, tears still rolling down my face. I wanted to explain it away, to say he swore to serve me as his empress and that came with certain risks. Had that not been so, he wouldn't have gone on my errand, but somewhere deep inside, the truthful answer to her question lingered.

My aunt shook her head. "No. He went because of his love for you and your father before you. He is loyal to his very end, and he will recover." She squeezed my hands. "Night is falling. You need to get some rest."

It was only in that moment that I realized how long I'd been at his side, only then that I regained some sense of time. The day had left, and twilight had descended.

"I can't," I said in a thin voice.

She pulled me to my feet and gave me a hard stare. "Solarynne is here with Corwyn. There is a bed in the room across the hall. I've slept there many nights since you departed for the High Cloud Courts. I will watch over Thalaj so you may rest a couple of hours."

An objection bubbled up my throat, but Nadia cut me off, insisting that I go. In her command, I saw everything that my mother had once been, and I relented. After a warm embrace, I relented to both my aunt's will and my exhaustion. As I crossed the room toward the door, I peered back at Thalaj.

Sleep then on my mind, I startled when Sentei Summergale stepped inside just as I reached for the handle.

"Kōgō." He waited again by the rules of decorum.

I sighed at the address, feeling a need to write this

tradition out of our culture, but it was my burden to accept. I motioned for him to continue.

"Zafrynne," he said. "The spellcaster, she will be here at dawn, and we can instruct her on what we need in the way of golems."

A glance back at Nadia reinforced her resolve for me to rest. "Very well," I said. "Please wake me when she arrives."

In the bed across the hall, I prayed briefly to the moon goddess, Selene, that she watch over us from high in the night sky. I threw the covers off in one moment, then pulled them back around me in the next. An hour, maybe more, passed. Finding sleep seemed impossible as I tossed from side to side. Finally, I found comfort on my back and counted my breaths, slowing them by measures until I fell into a fitful dreamscape.

Everything from the last few months swarmed in my mind and blended into pictures that made little sense. Alto-Trea danced with my mother. Corwyn fell to his death beside a table, yet we weren't in Nadia's cottage. Rather this happened at a feast upon the cloud island, in the High Cloud Court. My father cried red tears over my mother's pyre. Tsanseri battered Thalaj until he became unrecognizable. My sisters and their first advisors mingled in the temple where I'd communed with the Gods. Nadia, Solarynne, and the rest of the council performed upon the mountain's top, and a tree grew high above me, raining down its flowers as I rested in the grass. A crackling came in the distance, growing louder and louder. A creak sounded and a thud, and I shot upright in the bed.

"Kōgō," the healer's nasally voice called, and I peeled my eyes open. The gloaming of morning cast a gray hue over the room, and the birdlike healer stood in the open door. "Zafrynne has arrived."

◇◇◇◇◇◇◇◇◇◇◇◇◇◇

SCRUBBING BOTH HANDS OVER my face, I worked to gather my sleepy thoughts and banish the odd images that had littered the dream. My mind only dallied there for a moment before I pushed the covers aside and landed on my feet, and headed for the room across the hall. The healer stood aside allowing me to pass, but I sensed him at my back as I opened the door and found Nadia still sitting beside a resting Thalaj.

"Kōgō."

"Would you just speak already?" I snapped, turning to the sentei. I tired of the honorific and the waiting for my acknowledgment, longing for simple, straightforward speech. "For now, I excuse you from such formality. When this is all said and done, we may return to it."

A cloud drifted over his face—dismay at my outburst most likely—but he recovered quickly. He tipped his head forward and with a mite less assurance in his voice, he said, "Rest." He wrung his hands. "Gensui Thalaj Northerngale has rested well all night. You were right to sleep."

I inhaled, attempting to level myself. The reaction was wrong, I knew, but I was little more than a youngling myself, and my impatience was inevitable. I had to make amends, but I found it hard to let go of my frustration. Holding my breath helped, and once it had eased from my lungs, I said, "I am very sorry, Sentei." My reasons for snapping danced in my mind behind those words, but I left it at that. He had no need of explanation, and I didn't care to wash away the sentiment through further explanation.

"Well." He nodded. "I will have Teralynne watch over your guard until the three of us have spoken with

Zafrynne. He won't wake until much later today, so you have plenty of time to return before then." The healer left.

Nadia stood, crossed the room to me, and silently folded me into her arms. The embrace soothed me like nothing else possibly could in the moment. "Sentei Summergale is right. Thalaj rested the night with nothing but the gentle rise and fall of his shoulders as he breathed."

"It sounds like he found the rest I searched for long and hard."

"But you slept?" She pulled back, looking me over.

"I did. Not well, but I did."

"It is something."

The healer and Teralynne, the girl who had helped him tend to Thalaj the day before, returned. She took the chair at the bedside while Nadia and I followed Sentei Summergale down the hall, past the front room and the room where they'd set Thalaj's leg the day before, around a corner to the right, and down a long corridor. The healer opened the door and a gust of warmth rushed out.

Inside a narrow and lengthy room with a kettle brewing in a stone hearth, a long table sat centered under herbs hung to dry from the ceiling. A wispy woman with heavy silver hair sat at one end of the table dressed in simple black robes, the hood resting on her curved back. The healer introduced us to Zafrynne Keeningale. She didn't stand immediately, didn't offer me the respect that the others had. She merely glanced down into her cup and then back to the three of us and said, "I'll put on more tea."

Had I not watched her gather the herbs from the

plants drying above, I wouldn't have accepted the cup from her hand. But since she had, and since the sentei took a first sip, I accepted graciously and joined the gathering at the table. The healer told Zafrynne what we required in the way of golems.

She replied, "How many?"

"Ten," I answered without hesitation. I'd counted those I wished to protect yesterday upon learning of this as an option.

Her brow arched in question. "Are you certain that none of the ten are responsible for the malady already befallen the Dawnsgale?"

Glancing first at Nadia, then the healer, I allowed the suspicion to rest for a moment and asked, "How do you know it's a Dawnsgale?"

"Rumors, my young kōgō," she said, her voice sounding almost dusty, like it had dried out over decades of living in an arid climate. Maybe she'd spent too much time in a room much like this, where the fires burned constantly and smoked herbs for use in potions. She raised a brow. "Again, you are certain that none of the ten is a culprit?"

Sinking onto the bench, I tipped the cup and drank the minty warmth. It both energized and calmed me as soon as I'd swallowed the last of it, and I inspected the bottom of the cup where the herbs stuck to the glazed stoneware. "I can be certain of very little right now, Zafrynne."

She grabbed my cup and while she studied the herbal remnants, said, "It can take me several of Otarr's cycles to complete one golem. The task for this golem is simple, though, so I'd say two days for each. I will need hair from each of the people you wish to have me animate in miniature form."

Nadia cleared her throat. "Very well. The first one goes to Mairynne." She reached over and tugged a few hairs from my head.

"Ouch." I stared at my aunt, considering how strange of her to react so suddenly. Rubbing the spot where she'd plucked the hairs from my scalp, I added, "Nadia's and Corwyn's should follow. They've already fallen victim, and we need to prevent that from happening again. I'd like my sisters to each have one also. And Thalaj." As the last name fell from my lips, I tucked my chin, chagrin eating away at me for having already nearly lost him to whatever had happened at the Evernight Marshes.

"That is only six. A dozen days." Zafrynne said, seeming distant as she still examined the bottom of my cup.

I considered her earlier warning and what I knew about my sisters' first advisors. The final two I'd planned were for Mother Feathergale and Dorynne, but they posed no threat, so who would poison them? Unfortunately, I couldn't reckon what threat Nadia or Corwyn would pose either. After a moment, I resigned myself to the immediate family, Thalaj, and Corwyn. "I think that'll be enough for now." Thalaj may not even consider using the golem taster, but I felt I owed him a debt, and if he'd be recovering in Stormskeep as I had planned, he might need equal protection. I'd made the list and would leave it at that . . . for now. "Do you do this often?" I asked the woman.

"Never. Only during my training many long years ago." She took her gaze from inside my cup and stared upward, then shivered and looked back at me with a half-smile. "I only do it for you now because you are kōgō," she said, finally putting the cup down on the table with a thunk that reminded me of Thalaj's leg bone sliding back into place.

I quivered too. "I will ensure my counselors pay you well for your efforts." The words had no sooner left my mouth than I felt their emptiness echoing back to me. Zafrynne must have a reason for not performing such an enchantment since she'd learned how to do so, and the shudder she emitted led me to believe the endeavor might be dangerous. If it could harm, would gold truly compensate for her efforts?

Zafrynne reached across the table and grasped my arm at the wrist. I struggled to pull away but couldn't free myself from her grip. Her eyes fluttered closed, and she said in a distant voice, "Your travels shall twist and wind. Mayhap you have found your place, but your road has yet to reach the end. Friend and fiend, you'll encounter aplenty, but not until you plummet into the depths will you discover your soul's twin." Then, just as suddenly as she'd grasped my hand, she released it. Her eyes opened, and she smiled. "The leaves say many things, but this is all that they'll allow me to tell. I should return to begin my work."

Speechless, I watched as she stood and hobbled from the room.

NINE

A Man in Gray

KARYNNE RETURNED TO THE castle around midday, stating to those of us still gathered in the House of Healing that she'd carry news of our situation to the advisory council on my behalf. I thanked her with a tight hug and returned to my guard's bedside. Late that afternoon, Thalaj groaned. I turned and leaned over him as he opened his eyes. Confusion then worry darkened his gaze as he searched my face.

"Shhh," I said. "All is well. You'll be fine, and I have the totem we'll need to find the Tsinti." The small figurine had a loop attached, and I had hung it beside the stones at my neck. I reached up and pulled the necklace from my bodice to show him. When he seemed to relax, I added, "Right now is your time to rest and recover."

He scanned his battered body and tested how it

moved, issuing a grunt here and there, but he huffed loudly when he looked under the covers at his casted leg.

In the days that followed, Corwyn and Thalaj healed together, and I never left the House of Healing. On the sixth day after meeting Zafrynne, a messenger came with a package wrapped in brown paper and a rough rope securing it with a tight little knot. The healer offered me a knife to cut away the ties, and we examined the little golems. They looked so much like each of us, it was shocking. We explained the situation to Thalaj and Corwyn and how these would taste anything we wished to consume. Supposedly, they'd turn solid black if the food was of danger to our bodies or health. The spellcaster had keyed the golems to our unique person, so if something would be poisonous to one, but not the other, the golems would know.

Each came in a little box with a silver latch that we could carry securely within a pocket, though walking about with an animated miniature of myself gave me significant pause. Zafrynne had also delivered a potion of which Corwyn was to take three drops every morning as a measure to ward off his tremors. It seemed to work, and he improved more rapidly from the day he began his dosing.

I arranged for Mother Feathergale to have rooms prepared for Thalaj at the castle, and in another couple of days, we all returned to Stormskeep proper. Sentei Summergale came daily to check on Thalaj and Corwyn, but we had a plan—rest, recover, and have our food tasted by the miniature versions of ourselves. I went to Thalaj each morning, and we walked to Nadia's cottage at the beginning, middle, and ending of each day, visiting and taking our meals with Nadia and her partner. Corwyn healed quickly as the days passed. Nadia taught me to prepare food from her garden, and as such, when we ate there, we had to use our golems less than if we were to dine elsewhere. I attended to her cooking lessons eagerly under the assumption that I would have need of the skills before long.

Beyond preparing our own meals, we spent some time testing our tiny replicas. The bright orange lily flowers that Nadia tended, adding beauty to her garden, were poisonous when consumed. We brewed some of those and fed the resulting broth to the golems. They each turned a putrid gray, then blackened and fell over with a tiny choking sound. Then, like a dead plant coming back to life with a good soaking, they stood up before our eyes. Though it was a morbid game, we all laughed as the four tiny animated figurines went rigid, fell, and bloomed again. They were like new toys, and we behaved as younglings would and repeated the process several times, chuckling with amusement when their health returned.

Thalaj, ill accustomed to being so limited physically, grew increasingly frustrated with the rigid boot and restrictions imposed by Sentei Summergale. He maintained a grateful demeanor while a guest at my aunt's table, but on our walks, he repeatedly grumbled and complained. Roryn and another guard, Gaelynne, the one I'd seen him spar with in the yards, visited. It refreshed his mood slightly that he had the chance to learn about Stormskeep's protection and offer strategy and advice. When, after long weeks, he could walk without my assistance or leaning onto a cane, the healer removed the cast. Encouraging him to rest once he no longer wore the brace was near impossible, but he still attended meals on occasion at the cottage and kept his golem tucked in the breast pocket of his tunic at all times.

One evening, Thalaj had gone beyond Arashi's gates and returned with a hare. He and Corwyn worked together to skin and clean it for the pot, and Nadia and I prepared it for the evening meal. We sat down to eat, each holding a steaming bowl of the well-herbed meaty stew with root vegetables from the cottage garden. When we'd each sated our appetites, I leaned back in my chair with a goblet of sweet wine in hand.

Looking at the satisfied company, I felt comfortable enough to broach the subject. "Thalaj is gaining strength by the day. He's almost back to his full training schedule. I've spoken with Karynne about the party she's gathered to search for Father, and they should be preparing to leave the next time Selene is at her fullest in the sky." I took a drink, then added. "I will be traveling with them."

Corwyn dropped his goblet on the table and sat forward. "Mairynne, that journey is a tough fate for anyone. I fear you're not suited for it."

Sitting straighter, I said, "I am."

My near uncle persisted, "Kōgō, I mean no disrespect. But we do not know what this journey entails. Your parents sheltered you within the castle for your entire life, and you are now the Nantai empress, heaven's sovereign. The people of all the castes look to you and your council for guidance and decisiveness."

Corwyn was my subject. I could silence any objection and simply declare that this would come to pass. After all, it would. Knowing all this and that the right was mine left me with a temptation that seemed childish, so I stifled any comment. I'd felt this way since the day my father vanished. Each time I thought of him, the stone about my neck burned. Ever since the potion woman, Zafrynne, told me that the road before me stretched for lengths untold, I had never been more certain of my path. "Corwyn, you misplace your worry. The duties of the Nantai ruler are better handled by someone more mature than me." I paused, looking toward my aunt. "I've learned a great deal from Nadia during this recovery. Thalaj will be at my side along with other soldiers, so I will be safe. When I return, it will be with my father, I am certain."

He bowed his graying head. "Have you considered that Tennō Atheryn may not still live? It is so unlike him to be absent from his duties. His love for Nantai and her people was so great that he'd have sooner perished than remain away." A substantial weight sank upon Corwyn as he said these words, and it was clear that they tasted sour on his tongue.

Nadia reached across the table, took his hand, and turned to me. "All he says makes sense, Mairynne. That more than four moons have passed and your father hasn't appeared lead me to believe he will not return."

I grasped the stones about my neck. The one that rested in the center burned my palm, reassuring me in my conviction. "The thought has occurred to me many times. In truth, the counselors have voiced the same logic and reasoning to me on several occasions. Yet I still sense his life force still walking this land. I believe with everything in my soul that he lives. And this—holding court and deciding small grievances of a farmer here or a hunter there, or listening to the advice of my father's council on the matter of our next festival—is not my place. The politicsand minutia are already wearing on me."

Thalaj sat silently at my side.

I continued, "My road travels to other places. Where I don't know just yet, but on the morrow, I will go to the Triad and write the decree."

A long silence stretched between the four of us at the table.

At last, I turned to my aunt. "You have cared for me more than anyone since my mother's death and Father's disappearance. You have been wise as my first advisor and taught me what I most needed. You've shown me the same love as my mother, and you offer me only wise advice in the way of ruling the people." I took a deep breath. "I will leave the temporary leadership of the Nantai to you. You will have to visit the High Cloud Court to take the oaths in the same manner I did, but you will have the golem, Corwyn will be at your side, Solarynne will assuredly become your first advisor, and I will send a letter to Tsanseri to help you through the proceedings."

I touched the metal cuff I still wore beneath my sleeve on the upper part of my right arm. The time had arrived for us to go, and thankfully, I received no argument then and there from Thalaj.

∞∞∞∞∞∞∞∞∞∞∞∞

IT WAS UNLIKELY THAT I had fully convinced Nadia or Corwyn my intentions were the best for all involved. For my part, worry also gathered in my heart that the decision might be wrong, but of the options, it felt the most right. I hugged Nadia with everything I had and left her standing in the doorway with Corwyn. Thalaj walked me back to the castle itself across the lush grasses, and I looked up at Selene's countenance face as we went.

We were about halfway through the return when he looked at me, a glint in his eye. "How do you feel about a longer walk tonight?"

"Sure," I agreed suddenly, thinking that my rooms would be stifling.

I raised my skirts and followed Thalaj down the stone steps. Selene shone brightly as she approached her fullness. That it seemed so close made my heart leap, but how long did we have remaining? Four, maybe five days?

At the base of the castle's steep walls, we strolled

beside the river.

Thalaj broke the silence after several minutes. "Since I've been back and you've had so many attempts on the lives of your family members, I am beginning to see the logic in you leaving."

I stopped, grabbed the crook of his arm, and turned him to face me. "Are you actually saying you want me to go?"

"No," he scoffed. "I'd much prefer it if I could take you somewhere safe and leave you there until I return."

I snorted—a horrible sound, but one showing exactly what I thought of his overprotective sentiment.

With a chuckle, he continued, "I didn't think you'd agree with the approach."

"So, stubborn though you are, you're learning," I teased, but in the deepest part of me, I welcomed his change of heart, even if it remained reluctant.

"Mairynne—"

"Wait? No Kōgō?" I needled him some more.

He raised a perfectly slanted brow and asked, "Do you wish for me to call you that?"

We shared a laugh. This man knew me almost as well as anyone, and of course I didn't relish the thought of him or anyone else calling me Kōgō.

We resumed walking, but his demeanor turned more serious with each step. "I think it's best if we limit the number of people who know you are going. Do you have to approach the entire Triad in order to write your decree?"

My brows drew together as I asked, "It's customary for the three Hallowgales to witness the writings of the emperor or empress. Do you have cause to suspect them in something?"

He shook his head. "Nothing specific. I'm just being conscientious. Is it possible to only have one? Is there one you are closer to than the others?"

"If I had to choose, I'd pick Tasmynne, the priestess of Selene. If you feel strongly about that, I'll only go to her tomorrow."

"I do. I think it's a wise idea."

"What about the council? And my sisters? I'll need to share with them my intentions so they can help to make the arrangements for Nadia's ascension."

"I don't think you should tell them your plans. They would know soon enough after you're gone." He hesitated, then went on, "Tell me, have you given the little people to your sisters?"

"Do you mean the golems?" I smiled. The animation of the little clay-based replica of him bothered him more than he obviously wanted to admit.

"Yes. The golems." He sneered as he spoke the word, as if it tasted sour on his tongue. "Did you give them to Karynne and Yasmynne?"

"I haven't." My brows grew heavy at this. "I'm not sure what keeps me from giving them their protection. Maybe it's that I'll have to explain the entire situation. Or, it could be that the potion woman warned me from giving out the little tasters. I don't believe that either of my sisters had a hand in Corwyn's fate, but something . . . some weird intuition . . . tells me not to." As I said this, the cold stone about my neck grew colder.

Thalaj inhaled and huffed. "I worry that your intuition may be better than you know, and I'm not certain I can fathom what that means for you, for them, or for this journey we're about to take."

"And I think I worry that something further might happen to Nadia."

He turned to me. At what point we'd stopped, I couldn't say, but we stood under the moonlight next to the rushing water, and he looked at me darkly. "If you will allow it, I will assign Roryn and Gaelynne to guard your aunt and her partner." He looked away, then back to me with a slight smile.

My heart expanded with gratitude, but something else niggled inside. "What are you not saying, Thalaj?"

"I'd need to share the situation . . . and your plans . . . with my guards to help them be better prepared."

I broke away and trod a path back and forth at the water's edge. With one hand wrapped around my waist, my free hand worried at my bottom lip as I considered the possibility of sharing this information with people I barely knew in the place of people I'd spent my entire life around. Why did I feel more comfortable with the former rather than the latter? I couldn't pinpoint it, but when I looked up at my first guard, all I said was, "Make it happen."

He nodded. "One more thing . . ."

I went back to him and looked up into his dark eyes.

He glanced up at the moon, then resumed eye contact. "Selene will show her full body in the sky on the third night hence. I will come for you that morning in the early hours before dawn. Be prepared to meet me and leave before first light."

◇◇◇◇◇◇◇◇◇◇◇◇◇◇◇

THE PROMINENT CHARACTERISTIC OF the moon goddess's

temple was the sizable quarter moon-shaped cutout in the ceiling designed for watching the goddess pass through the night skies. I found Tasmynne, priestess of Selene, there and pulled her from gathering tithes people had placed upon the goddess's altar.

"Tasmynne, I have need of you within the grand sanctuary." I latched onto her hand and pulled her forward.

"Kōgō, with due respect, what is this regarding? I have duties I must attend to before nightfall and the service this evening."

"I need you to bear witness."

Upon her hand, the moon-shaped ring gleamed . . . with the sigil of the goddess.

"Have you gathered Edamyn and Arlyn as well?"

"Your holiness"—I stopped and turned to face her nose to nose—"I won't be bringing them into this matter. While that is customary, it is not a requirement. The annals only require one Hallowgale to witness an official decree. I'd like to keep this one as quiet as possible for now. Can I trust you with this?"

Her eyes widened, and when she gave a jerky nod, I pulled her forward. I stopped outside the large open doors and looked around for others before searching the sanctuary inside. When I'd satisfied myself that no others were present, I went to the dais that held the most current of the annals. I picked up the feathered quill and dipped it into the ink. Weighing my words, I penned the date, then wrote:

I, Kōgō Mairynne Evangale, decree that upon my realized absence from the city of Arashi and Stormskeep Castle, my aunt and sister to

the murdered Kōgō Noralynne Evangale shall
ascend to the Serpentine Throne. In doing so,
she shall recite Morwyn's oath, declaring that
the throne shall return to its previous owner
should that owner return.

I signed the decree and handed the quill to Tasmynne.

The priestess read my words, then lifted her eyes to meet mine. "I cannot sign this, Kōgō."

"Your holy vows bind you to this duty." I pushed the quill closer.

Tasmynne took it and signed. I retrieved the black waxed candle from the altar and dripped wax next to her name. She stared at the moon ring on her right hand for a long minute until I reached forward and took her by the wrist. She didn't resist but didn't actively aid in sealing the decree either. After she'd completed the imprint, I let out a sigh just as the scuffling sound of boots alerted us to someone's approach.

We both looked up, and I closed the book as my new attendant, Dorynne, appeared in the door. She panted, but said between breaths, "Oh, good, I found you Kōgō Mairynne." She stopped and gulped, then added, "Ohmyn Havengale and Idalynne Feathergale sent me in search of you."

That seemed an odd combination, but I ignored the inclusion of the counselor Havengale as I moved toward my newest attendant, "What would put Mother Feathergale in mind to send you in such a rush for?"

Dorynne, having recovered her breath some, looked at her shoes and wrung her hands. "She just said to bring you to the council chambers quickly."

I pressed my lips into a tight line. "Tasmynne, will

you find Edamyn and Arlyn and meet us there?"

The priestess curtsied. "Right away, Kōgō."

Without further conversation, I exited the sanctuary. Once outside and connected to the atmosphere, I called the wind to speed my journey. The bridge emptied on the same level of the keep as the library and my chambers. I quickly climbed the steps to the next level and hurried into the council chambers where the Serpentine Throne awaited. Inside, Ohmyn stood beside a guard who held a sword on someone in gray nondescript clothing sitting upon his knees and facing the throne.

I couldn't see his face from where I stood.

Mother Feathergale paced along the other side of the throne, and when she noticed me, she rushed forward. "Mairynne, we found him trying to enter your rooms, and he carried a phial in his hand."

A phial?

My rooms?

I looked beyond the woman I'd known all my life to the gray form on the floor and moved. I couldn't feel my legs and could no longer hear the Sundai Falls for the blood rushing in my ears. "Do you have the phial?" I asked to no one or to anyone; I didn't care which.

Mother Feathergale scurried behind me. "Havengale does."

Suspecting, or mayhap fearing, what I would see, I extended a hand. My counselor placed a corked glass phial on my open palm. When I examined the fluted red flower within, my heart turned to stone.

I passed the slender bottle back to Ohmyn made a point of not looking at anything except the Serpentine Throne—that accursed chair that represented a duty I hadn't wanted. But now it represented the ability to rain down justice on someone who had wronged my family twice over and taken my best friend's life. Mayhap this person had intended to poison me, and as such became a traitor to the throne, to my family, to the Storm Sorcerers, and to Nantai herself. When I reached the steps, I climbed slowly and at the top I turned with my chin held high and sat.

A pair of guards appeared in the doorway through which I'd just entered.

I projected my voice. "One of you, go to Sentei Summergale and bring him here to me. Ohmyn Havengale has something for him to examine. Tell him the empress believes it'll be primlock."

After they disappeared, I finally settled my gaze on the gray form cowered before me. He lifted his eyes, and within them, I took note of a white speck within his right pupil. The eyes looked youthful but peered back from within an aged face. If this man were to stand, he would stoop. In truth, his back was bent where he knelt upon the floor.

My voice sounded hollow, distant, and cold as I spoke. "You wished me well when I offered you a piece of my mother, yet you hold ill will against me for some reason I do not follow."

He remained silent, but a smile spread on his face.

"Do you have nothing to say for your actions?" Anger began to filter into my words.

"I do not," he answered, a defiant note within the once again hale voice—the sound so very at odds with the aged man.

"But you poisoned Jessamynne Feathergale?"

Silence.

"And Corwyn Dawnsgale.?"

Nothing.

I leaned forward. "If you choose not to answer to these charges, I will take that as an answer of affirmation. Now. I will ask once more."

Guards trickled into the room at the back and lined the walls.

I disregarded them. "Did you poison my attendant and my aunt's consort?"

The gray-dressed man, both old and young at the same time, with the fleck in his right eye, pressed his lips together and remained mute.

Ohmyn Havengale shook his head, then stopped, his cheeks still blubbering for a second following. "Should we have him sent to the cells beneath the keep to await his death?"

No matter that he'd likely poisoned two people I loved dearly, the thought of asking someone else to slaughter him soured my stomach. "No."

I paused for long enough that those who'd entered the room began to murmur.

I raised both hands. "Let's put him in the cell within the highest spire. The cold will be upon us soon, and nature can take her course upon this traitor."

I stood and walked slowly to the door of the throne room, between the guards, and turned toward my rooms. After descending the stairs, I called a gust of wind to see me quickly to my chambers. Within, I locked the door and went to my dresser. Grabbing onto the bowl sitting on top with shaky hands, I emptied the few contents of my stomach over and over again until I felt weak but purged of having sentenced someone to a slow death.

Again, the truth rang in my ears as to how I wasn't fit to be an empress. I hadn't the stomach for such things.

TEN

Into the Gloaming

AWAKE IN THE WEE morning hours on the third day since I'd strolled with Thalaj and two days after I'd penned the decree and sent the man to the spire. I bustled quietly around my chambers gathering the items I'd collected surreptitiously over the last days. Though I'd laid in bed for what seemed the longest night of my life, I hadn't slept. I felt some relief that the guards had apprehended the culprit who'd poisoned Corwyn, yet my nerves still bundled in my stomach and spun anticipation throughout my mind. At the cleaning table, beside the basin, I filled a water skein from the pitcher Mother Feathergale had filled late yesterday, also at my behest. I didn't know how early she and Dorynne would arrive to prepare for the day, but after every item I packed, I went to the front of my rooms to check for their arrival, hoping that Thalaj would come before.

With my pack sealed, I stepped onto the balcony but remained close enough to the secret passageway to hear a knock. The crisp air chilled my skin, and across the sky, the full moon hung above the spires of the citadel, a yellow halo within the deep purple night. At odds with the stillness of the predawn hours, blood raced through my veins, a steady pulse beat in my ears, and I fidgeted as I waited.

I twitched at every sound and jumped when the small scratching sound startled me from inside, a noise a rodent would make as it pawed at the ground for grubs. But it wasn't an animal; it came from behind the art that hid the secret passage. I went.

When I opened the hidden door, Thalaj was holding an orb of dancing bluish lightning high to light the dark stairwell. "Get your things. It's time."

I retrieved my pack and returned. Stepping inside, I pulled the painting closed and tried to turn in the tight space.

Thalaj stopped me so he could appraise my pack, then gave a small satisfied smile, and asked, "You have the totem?"

I grasped the end of the throng hanging at my neck. It had remained there since my time at the House of Healing, a token as important as the ones that represented the souls of my parents. At my nod, he turned. I held a hand on the wall to steady myself as we descended countless stairs. Outside, under Selene's watch, I called the wind and lowered us to the grass behind a copse of trees. Thalaj scanned the area, tilted his head, and made for the city's gates. We moved precisely as planned and would meet the remainder of the party at Stormskeep's exit. Not another person stirred within the streets at the gods-forsaken early hour. Thalaj walked with purpose, in silence, but glanced over his shoulder several times to ensure I kept pace. He deftly maneuvered through the narrow cobbled streets, past the House of Healing, around homey neighborhoods, and between the shops at the market. It seemed he could make this way blindfolded. For my part, I couldn't break concentration long enough to ask questions though they stirred in my agitated mind.

When we arrived at the stables, I slowed, expecting that we'd meet the others inside and gather horses for the journey. Thalaj turned back to me, grabbed my wrist, and pulled me forward.

I resisted. "Aren't we meeting the others?" I asked.

"I sent word to the others last night to meet here at seventh bell. I plan to be well away before that hour. Pull up your hood and come on."

Beyond the stables, facing the guardhouse, I stopped. "What about the guards? Didn't you just mention that our departure would be in secret."

Thalaj rounded back on me and pulled me into the shadows. "I've staffed the night watch with only those I trust. Roryn and Gaelynne lead the shift."

I shifted my gaze uncertainly.

"What is it, Mairynne?" he asked, clearly growing short with my reluctance.

"Maybe . . ." I started.

He quirked a brow.

"Maybe this isn't the best idea," I admitted. In the depths of my soul, I knew it was my path, that I was meant to travel this road, and that this journey was what Zafrynne had spoken of when she read my fate in the herbs. So why, as I stood on the very precipice, did I fear what we faced?

Thalaj sighed. "Mairynne, your determination persuaded even me, so you're not turning back now. But time is important; your doubts will wait until we're at a safe distance."

"What if we're discovered?"

"It's early enough that no one will know immediately, and I trust my guards to keep this quiet until after someone notices your absence in the castle. It will take several hours." He pressed his lips together, then narrowed the distance between us and lowered his voice. "What you're feeling is what the Frost Fighters call the spirit of home's hearth. It's fear of facing something you don't know, but you've convinced even me of your need to go, and as the one charged with your very protection, I've the most reason for objection."

Glancing down, I said, "But what if this is exactly what Father did and never returned?"

"Do you really believe that?" He raised his brows.

I shook my head. If Father had left willingly, he would have come back to his duty and his people. The stone burned the delicate skin beneath my shift, emphasizing the rightness of my conclusion.

"Then trust me, and you'll be better by the time we enter the forest."

After another doubtful thought, I decided to put away my misgivings, pulled my hood over my head, and gave him the trust he'd earned by his service to me and my father before.

At the guardhouse, Roryn smiled widely. He and Thalaj clasped arms.

Thalaj asked, "Do you have them?"

"Aye, we do," the guard answered.

Gaelynne stepped forward with a belt holding two holstered scimitynes—weapons I knew well from having observed my first guard wield them in the training yards. Others used short or longer straight swords based on their fighting styles, and some fought with daggers or a longbow. My first guard was the only one who dared use the small curved blades as a weapon. I expected he'd strap the belt at his waist, but the three guards turned to me. I looked from face to face, unclear of their expectation.

Gaelynne guffawed after seeing my reaction. "Lift your cloak, Kōgō." The woman stood taller than both Thalaj and Roryn and wore her hair cut bluntly at her chin. I'd seen her before but never this close. Her forehead was a bit too broad for her face, but her mouth was soft. Her bold laugh made me like her immediately, and I did as she said. She strapped the belt at my waist and stepped back. "Don't take those out until someone shows you what to do with them. I'd hate to see you lose a hand or something worse."

I nodded. Of course, I would need something for protection, but it would have made more sense to give me something easier to use. Reality set in. My journey had started, and I was going alone into the world with only Thalaj. My heart patter could have been from thrill or anxiety—which, I couldn't tell. We walked past the gates that had held my entire life up until that moment as Otarr's first light painted a line across the horizon. We veered to the right, met the northern branch of the Sundai River, and followed it south.

A sense of freedom I'd imagined for months settled over me, and feelings of—not happiness, but something for which I had no accurate words lightened my steps. A truth, mayhap. But that seemed a weak explanation. At the very least, it contained purpose.

And my purpose felt right.

Mayhap it was my imagination, but on the wind, I heard my father's voice.

Truth to thine self first.

Thank you for reading

Call of the Storm Sorcerer

The Serpentine Throne Book One

Other books in the series

Call of the Syrensea; May 17, 2021

Call of the Ryu Dragon; June 21, 2021

Call of the Scorched Empire; July 19, 2021

Call of the Maelstrom; August 23, 2021

For a free legend from The Serpentine Throne world, news on upcoming releases, promotions, and more, sign up for my newsletter here:

https://bit.ly/susanstradiottosnewsletter

OR

If you'd like to be a part of my street team to preview and review my books when they launch, sign up here:

https://bit.ly/SusansStreetTeam

OR

Continue reading for the first chapter of

Call of the Syrensea

The Serpentine Throne Book Two

ONE

Beyond Arashi, Nantai

MUSCLES BURNED AND BUNCHED within my calves. A pack bounced on my shoulders. Scimityne scabbards thudded against my legs with every step, a new thing I'd accepted from the guard Gaelynne, who had helped us escape. They held weapons Thalaj had crafted specially for me and, as such, something I would treasure always. My skirts rustled over the grasses of the vale, growing heavy and damp with predawn dew. My heart and legs pumped in concert.

Away from all I'd ever known, I ran.

The moon goddess, Selene, neared the end of her watch in the westward skies, but the sun god, Otarr, had yet to brighten the mountainous horizon in the east.

Over my shoulder lay the city of Arashi, the only place I'd truly known in the passing of more than twenty summers. Since the time of Emperor Makenyn five long ages before, it'd been the Nantai's star city at the base of Mount Sundai. Held within Arashi's walls and beside the great waterfalls, Stormskeep Castle—home of the Serpentine Throne and the seat of emperors and empresses throughout the ages—watched over the city and the vale beyond.

Built around Sundai River Falls, Arashi had been where my father, Tennō Atheryn Evangale had ruled before his mysterious disappearance. The castle and city streets were where my sisters and I had played as younglings, learning the limits of our sorcery. Inside those walls, other young Storm Sorcerers and I had gathered in the citadel near the keep to learn from the Havengales—priests of our Holy Triad. Selene's priestess, Tasmynne, had told stories using painted boards to warn us of the dangers beyond Arashi's walls—the winged predators of the Rausu Mountains and the nekodai in the north. Both vicious birds and mammoth cats always thirsted for youthful blood in the tales. Younglings perished under beaks, claws, and fangs. The paintings on the storyboards had always been splattered with crimson blood, and though I'd clung to her stories, nightmares followed.

But for all the learning and despite the stories, I'd never seen the expanse of my country with my own eyes. There were so many people throughout Nantai I'd never met. Now, I ran toward them to find what I had lost—what Nantai had lost.

Father. Emperor.

Within Arashi, I had answered my duties and followed my father's decrees within the annals. Though I would have preferred otherwise, though the stones I wore around my neck called me away from the city, and though I hadn't been wise enough for such a mantle, I had ascended to sit upon the Dragonscale Throne. I'd become Empress of Nantai.

Kōgō Mairynne Evangale.

I'd seen my first guard and protector healed after his encounter with the Small Folk of the Evernight Marshes—a mission he'd tended on my behalf. Then, I'd sentenced my best friend's murderer to imprisonment within Stormskeep's spires. But on this morning after decreeing that Aunt Nadialynne Riversgale, my mother's twin sister, ascend to the throne during my absence, I answered the call of the stones I kept on a necklace near my heart. Through the vale, I escaped home and duty with my protector Thalaj in search of Father. Despite my sisters', my advisers', and the clergy's beliefs, within my heart and soul, I had no doubts. Atheryn Evangale, Tennō of Nantai, lived. And the throne rightfully belonged to him.

We ran as morning's twilight came.

With my storm-fed sorcery, I called the wind when I tired. Yet, after a time, my breathing steadied into a quicker rhythm as a renewed wave of energy flowed through my body.

Gloaming lifted.

Night retreated.

Behind us, the citadel's bells began to toll, awakening Arashi for the common daylight routines. Almost to the Yubar Forest at the edge of the vale, Thalaj stretched his step. I struggled to keep pace at his side while counting the gongs in my mind . . . four, five, six. A glance behind revealed sunlight kissing the top of Mount Sundai, setting the mists of the waterfalls aglow, turning Stormskeep's spires golden, then unfolding to cover the castle and the city itself. The stone wall fortifications protecting the city within gleamed under Otarr's light as his rays stretched from them across the valley, like arms brushing the moistened grass. We left a dark trail, but the sooner we reached the woods, the sooner we could more easily cover our tracks. Only moments before Otarr's bright eyes found us, I ducked under a low-hanging branch into the tree cover. Broad leaves and shadow welcomed us into the southernmost swath of the Yubar Forest.

Along with the city and my home, I left my doubts behind. The time for my adventure had come, and with it, the time for me to let go of my imperial duties. Between the city gates and the forest's edge, every step I'd taken had solidified my conviction. I would deliver my father back to his seat upon the Dragonscale Throne. It was a new duty, one I had chosen, and a band had released from around my chest. I had to trust in my peoples' traditions and that the decree I'd written would come to pass. Eventually, I would see Arashi again, but whether I'd remain at Stormskeep then and grow into the ruler my father believed me to be remained a worry for another day. This day, I pursued my own will.

Truth to thine self first, my father's voice echoed in my mind.

"Yes, Father," I whispered in agreement and pushed my legs harder.

Ahead, Thalaj stopped under the shade of broad leaves. When I arrived at his side, he relieved me of my pack, unlatched it, and tossed me a tunic and rough-spun pants. "Change. I estimate we have an hour to get as far into the forest as possible before the warnings go up." He turned away, giving me the privacy to do as he bade.

Once I'd dressed in simpler clothing and resecured my pack, we continued deeper into the Yubar Forest, shaded from Otarr's light by the tangled canopy above.

We trekked over decaying leaves, frogs croaking in the nearby wetlands along the river. While we'd left behind the roaring of the falls, the Sundai babbled gently and birds sang above. I'd been to the edge of the forest and just inside, but never this far within. Mother and Father hadn't allowed me to venture into its depths, warning that I would easily get lost or carried off by one of the wolf packs rumored to prowl the forest that stretched from the slope of the Rausu Mountains my people called home toward the Syrensea in the west. Aside from the paintings and storyboards, I'd never seen these wolves, and I'd often suspected the Hallowgales had invented the tale to keep younglings from wandering off.

The serenity under the trees allowed me to further contemplate this journey and allow my guard to do the same. I'd given him space thus far because I trusted him implicitly. But the original plan had been for him to go in search of Father with a small team of Storm Sorcerer guards. When the bells began to chime from the citadel again, quieter then as they were farther away, I skip-stepped and caught up to Thalaj, pulling him to a stop. "We're an hour into the forest. Tell me why we're going at this alone," I demanded, my words firm but lacking outrage. I had trouble putting forward a hard empress's façade when I felt a thrill to simply be free.

He slowed his pace but kept us moving. "In the Evernight, I was captured."

"I thought there was a fight, that you and Roryn—"

He shook his head. "I left Roryn in the camp while I went to retrieve the totem."

"You went in alone?" I asked, my eyes wide with surprise that he'd abandoned his only ally on the mission. "Rumor tells the Small Folk feed on our magic."

He nodded. "Aye, I entered alone. Though I am uncertain that bit about the Small Folk feeding on magic is true. I took a beating, but I'm better now." He cocked a half smile.

I shook my head. "I may never understand you, Thalaj Nightingale. You say you trust Roryn but you wouldn't work with him. Instead, you risk your life trying to what?"

He gave me a sidelong glance but refused me a believable answer. "It's simply who and *what* I am . . . how I trained." He stepped over a fallen branch and extended a hand to help me. "My methods are of little importance."

Huffing, I accepted his hand. "Had you perished in the foolish attempt, where would I be now? You are the one responsible for helping me away from Arashi."

He winced but dismissed my accusation. "Regardless of how I entered the marshes, I learned that we not only need to find the Tsinti, but we need to seek out their witch wife. To answer your question about why we left without a larger search party, I didn't believe we would have a hope of gaining entrance into a Tsinti camp if we brought a full traveling party. The Tsinti, themselves, are a private folk, only traveling under a *tsym*. We've spoken of this before. You know that they only reveal themselves to those they choose. It's why I went for the totem."

I fought an urge to reach for my necklace where the stones and the totem hung near my heart. "How will we know where to look?"

"I'm guessing a bit on that one, but they're a nomadic people. Nomads have a pattern, and I believe they will bring the silks from Yōtei in the east to the Southern Fork market in autumn."

My stomach flipped. "We're going to the Great Market?" For years, I'd begged Father to take us with them to the largest market in our lands, where everyone congregated along the southernmost fork of the Betsu River for the time between the two moons of the cooling season to share in news from every corner of Nantai and to trade.

"No. I wouldn't risk taking you into such a place."

I glared. "Why? I'll not trade the confines of Stormskeep for a travel companion who keeps me equally secluded."

The manner in which his look flitted to mine intoned many thoughts, amusement mayhap, but certainly exasperation. He chose to speak none of that. "If that had been my plan, I would have brought the travel party." He looked up at a bird calling above and whistled back. Amused, his eyes settled back on mine. "No. I plan to try to find the Tsinti in the Central Grasslands before they make their way down the Betsu."

"Oh." I slumped.

Thalaj gave a small laugh. "You're empress, Mairynne, and you have your majority now. Once we've concluded this quest, you may attend the market every year, and I will ensure your protection when you do."

We traveled in companionable silence for several minutes, then he added, "My hope is that alone, the Tsinti will welcome us into their caravan."

Otarr must have been high in the sky by the time we stopped by the river to eat. Even under the Yubar's shade, it grew hotter. I'd almost drained my waterskin, and relief struck me hard as we stopped for water. I sat on a boulder beside the babbling stream. Thalaj filled his skein, then reached for mine. As he held it in the clear, flowing waters, I lifted my hair. Holding my other hand forward, palm up, I found the center of my sorcery powers and gathered a breeze from the water surface to cool my face and neck.

Thalaj stood and plugged the cap back into place but then dropped the waterskin as a sound ripped through the sky. I shrank, sliding from my rock. My guard freed his scimitynes with a *schling* breaking the thick silence under the greenery. We both searched above for the source of the bone-chilling screech. While night had obscured the source before, trees did so then. Though after the sound, a rush of wind sent the treetops rustling and a rain of green leaves showered around us. Then . . . all went still once more. Whatever it had been had silenced the sounds of the Yubar. Frogs and birds alike paused.

I didn't breathe for long moments following, but when my guard seemed to release a bit of tension, I looked at him with wide eyes. "That thing. Whatever it is. Does it follow us? Have you heard it any time when we're not together?"

He came out of his crouch and slowly slid his weapons back into their homes. The birds chirped again, tentatively at first. Frogs joined in the chorus, resuming their rhythmic croak. The restored song seemed to signal safety had returned.

"No," Thalaj said simply.

While I'd been so certain of my journey only a couple of hours before, a part of me began to long for the protection of the castle's stone walls. "Should we—"

"No," he cut me off and turned a cold, arresting stare in my direction. "Mairynne, I have no idea what that is, but I'm not going to coddle you on this journey. We'll run into many things, and we'll face them together.

If some beast truly follows us, it will eventually have to do more than screech in the sky, and we'll manage the situation when that happens. Until then, it's out of our control."

I hesitated, fingered the warm stone about my neck, and slowly reached to touch the hilt of a *scimityne* at my hip. I stiffened. A resolution formed. Beyond Arashi's walls, I was no longer Lady Mairynne, not Princess, Empress, and certainly not Kōgō. Out here, I was simply Mairynne. A world of new experiences lay before me. Certainly, we'd face new challenges and obstacles, along with all the wonder of Nantai beyond the city where I'd come of age. I could no longer reach for the comfort and safety of all I'd known.

My hand grasping the small, curved sword's hilt, I looked up into Thalaj's dark features with a new wonder. "You'll teach me to use these?"

"Not today." He smiled, obviously reading the change in me. "Not today, but very soon. I will." He gathered my discarded water bladder and handed it to me, also helping me up from my reclined position against the rock. "Before nightfall, I'd like to make it to a small grove that marks the midpoint between Arashi and the edge of the grasslands. Tomorrow, we'll press forward to seek the Tsinti on the Central Grasslands. If they accept us, we'll have their tsym to protect us from sight, and I'll begin showing you the elementary moves."

◇◇◇◇◇◇◇◇◇◇◇◇◇◇◇◇

THE REMAINDER OF THE day passed as Thalaj and I hiked around trees, over fallen limbs, and southward. At our right side, the Sundai continued her path toward the Syrensea. A soft bed of decaying leaves cushioned our steps. Under our boots, sticks crackled from time to time, adding to the lullaby of the running water, rustling foliage, and chirping creatures. The light faded, green seemingly growing thicker, as the day moved toward night once again.

"If I am not mistaken, where the river bends just ahead is the clearing," said Thalaj. He looked toward the bend and up into the leafy ceiling. "Perhaps there will be enough light remaining to catch a fish for an evening meal."

When we broke through the edge of the trees, we saw a clearing reminiscent of the scene from the Cloud Courtier performance of the legend of Sosano and Inara beside the river. Small flowers nestled amid wispy grasses with the last rays of Otarr streaming down. Mist drifted into the clearing, thickening. I wondered what the delicate grasses would look like when morning's dew wept from their blades.

Thalaj dropped his pack at the trunk of a large tree and said, "Aahhh, yes. A blessed fog," seeming relieved of a worry I couldn't fathom. When I looked at him questioningly, he answered, "It will provide cover enough that a fire won't be visible from afar. Gaelynne and Roryn were to send the Arashi guards farther west, toward the North Sundai, but if any other search party has picked up our trail, the mist should help keep us out of sight."

He gathered dry sticks and fallen limbs from beneath the trees and stacked them carefully, then stood and placed his hands on his hips above his weapon belt, some hidden thoughts alive in his mind as he regarded me.

"It is disquieting when you look at me so," I said, dancing around asking directly what he thought. Thalaj had been a fixture in Stormskeep, always near and watching over our family. He had been young when he came to Arashi and dedicated himself to my father. To this day, I am uncertain he'd gained his majority at the time he joined the Arashi guard. I'd been younger still. Mayhap it had been Father's direction to watch over me, but from the beginning we shared an easy, comfortable friendship. Only in the times nearing my mother's death had a hint of something more begun to surface. This would be the first of many nights where we'd be alone together. My purpose out here had little to do with Thalaj, but I couldn't think of another person I'd prefer to have at my side. Despite that I wished for more connection, there was naught suggestive in the purse of his lips as he considered.

In an instant, he grinned boyishly. "How would you like to learn to catch a fish?"

I wrinkled my nose at first, then changed my mind and shrugged. Anywhere beyond a city, the skill might be of use. And I had no inkling of when I might return to the city. The taller grass blades tickled my palm as I crossed toward Thalaj and the forest. He squatted, retrieved a line from his pack, and grabbed a thinner, greener stick from those he'd collected and tested how it bent. When he seemed satisfied, he tilted his head toward the river and began walking. I left my pack with his beside our camp at the clearing and followed him back toward the Sundai. Upon the banks, Thalaj passed me the line and stick, then crouched again, removed his boots, and rolled his breeches to his knees. With bare feet, Thalaj stepped into the shallow waters. He hissed. The waters flowing from Mount Sundai were colder than even he—as half Frost Fighter—had expected. Dipping his hands into the shallow water, he reached deeper several times and then stood with a tiny fish writhing between his fingers. From his belt, he produced a barbed piece of metal.

I winced when he stabbed it through the baby fish, regretful for the small animal's fate. I said a quick prayer to Atun for the life given so that we might hunt for our next meal.

Thalaj took the end of the line from me and tied it around the metal. As he tied the other end of the line to the stick, he nodded to my boots. "You'll want to take those off to keep them dry."

With my legs bare too, I joined him in the water. Indeed, it was icy upon my feet and ankles, and I entered much slower than my guard.

As I reached his side, he handed me the wider end of the stick and pointed. "See the dark pool there? That's where the fish will be." He made motion as if he still held the stick. "Swing the stick and aim the line there."

I tried once, but got the barb snagged in my breeches. Laughter—a rare thing from Thalaj—surrounded us as he freed my inadvertent catch. Afterward, he demonstrated a better technique. When the line settled between us and the dark pool he'd mentioned, he handed the stick back to me.

"What now?" I asked.

He folded his arms over his chest and answered, "We wait."

In a matter of moments, the stick started jiggling in my hands.

"Oh . . . oh . . . oh, what do I do?" I stammered.

"Pull back."

I did.

It jerked and pulled.

"Good. Now just hold." He reached for the line, swiping twice before he captured it and pulled. It took several tries, but he wrestled a fish the size of his forearm out of the water. "To the shore," he barked, already moving in that direction.

I hurried over, my eyes wide and curious.

With the silvery fish lying in the grass and gaping to breathe, Thalaj pulled the barb from its mouth, removed the smaller fish, and tucked the metal back into his belt. I snarled as he reached a finger inside the fish's mouth and lifted it. "Well done, for your first time," he teased.

Near camp, the fog had thickened while we fished. Thalaj cleaned the scales from the fish and swiped his knife along the bones, pulling away chunks of white meat. The light was near gone as he handed the skewered meat to me and built a fire. The fish, smoky from the fire, near melted on my tongue. Afterward, we sat shoulder to shoulder watching the flames die down. Autumn and cooler days would soon be upon us, but that night still felt warm.

Eventually, Thalaj offered me a blanket upon which to sleep and spread out his own.

I stood and once again imitated his more experienced ways. As I finished preparing my pallet, the hairs on my arms rose and a shiver ran down my spine as a rustle in the grasses sounded.

"An empress . . ." a haunting voice, as if borne by the mist itself, began from within the fog.

I reached for my sorcery and called the wind to push the haze away, but it simply swirled. The flames flickered, threatening to extinguish our only light, so I released the gust.

The voice continued, ". . . alone in the wild with but a single guard for her protection."

The ghost in the dark fog tsked thrice. The sound echoed.

The fog pushed and retreated as if it had grown tentacles engorged with sound.

"How very odd, these times we live in," the unseen voice finished.

Thalaj brandished his scimitynes, searching for the source. "Mairynne," he hissed. "Grab your belt. Flip the buckle and pull one blade from the leather." When I had the small curved sword in hand and stared at the blade as if it were a serpent, he continued in hushed tones, "Face the honed edge away from your body and hold it in front of your chest. Like this."

My hand shook as I imitated him again.

He lowered his chin and came near enough I could feel his breath upon my cheek—cool as he clearly allowed his own source of power to surface. "Remember what I said? We'll face these things together."

I nodded.

"Now," he commanded, entirely having changed into the able captain of the empress's guard. "Stand with your back to mine. Where I turn, you turn. Keep your shoulders glued to mine and follow my lead as if this were a dance."

I bobbed my head and positioned myself.

"Show yourself!" my guard called into the mist.

A laugh, like funeral bells tolling, rang from within the dark mist, and the voice came again. "I do not wish her injury, half-breed."

My spine stiffened at the same slander I'd heard before from a voice I now also recognized. From deep within the center of my chest, I found my voice and enunciated every beat. "Alto-Trea. Do as Thalaj commands and show yourself."

The Cloud Courtier's face peeked from the mist, shoulders and hands apparent, but the lower half obscured. Though in the dark with a small glow from our campfire, Alto-Trea's visage seemed a replica of every one of the Courtier's caste I recalled from my ascension. As had been the case then, the only identification apparent was an emblem upon the shoulder.

The Swan.

It doubly confirmed the Courtier's identity.

Thalaj turned us so I faced away from Alto-Trea.

I made to move, but a wave of cold wafting from my guard stopped me. He hissed over his shoulder. "Keep tight. Others may be behind us." Then to the courtier, he said, "I would not judge you so reckless, Alto-Trea, to have come deeply into the forest at night. Alone. And for no purpose. You and others have brought a cloud island to this grove in search of something specific. Us, if I must guess. And surely you're not naïve enough to face me alone. Have the others reveal themselves as well."

Alto-Trea's voice remained even as he replied, "You seem parano—"

A shriek rang out in the distance, a sound I was growing to know all too well.

"—oid," the Courtier finished.

No longer heeding Thalaj's instruction to face away, I turned. Something that one might call a smile twitched at the corner of the courtier's perfectly illusion-drawn lips, yet it chilled my blood.

"What was that?" I demanded.

Neither voice nor demeanor changed as the Swan answered, "One day very soon, young Mairynne Evangale, you will learn."

Thalaj stepped in front of me. He stiffened his arms with his blades to either side, readying them as I'd seen him do so many times before he began a sparring match with one of the soldiers he trained. "Why not this night, Alto-Trea? It makes little sense to come to us with no purpose save to say 'one day...' "

A flash of blue lightning at the base of each scimityne, quickly lit then extinguished, signaled Thalaj held his magic just beneath his taut posture.

"And precisely why, half-breed, would an illusionist *not* have such an agenda?"

Bristling, I gathered breath to object. But the temperature around me plummeted, stealing my reaction.

Thalaj said, "I have no favor for illusionists. I will see your true form here and now, Cloud Courtier, once your body lies at my feet."

I lay a hand on my guard's arm. He didn't look over, but also didn't pounce into an attack. Violence would gain us no purchase with one of the illusionist caste, the ones who managed the political courts. And the fog was too thick. Alto-Trea remained half obscured, and though there wasn't another soldier in Arashi as fast as Thalaj, I doubted his strike would be fast enough. Lifting my chin, I asked, "*Is* that why you've come, Alto-Trea? It seems a long journey for something so small if you've brought down an island from the skies." I flourished a hand. "As clearly you have by this fog."

Alto-Trea pulled a thumb and middle finger to a point where a beard would be—if the Swan had chosen that as a guise. For reasons I couldn't connect, that simple movement seemed like the placement of another pawn in whatever strategy game this person played.

The Swan pulled back partway into the mist. "Wise,

youngling."

I bristled again but held myself in check.

The courtier continued, "But she will no longer hold me in favor if I share aught that would give you advantage. For this night, I shall bid you farewell."

The haze swallowed the Swan then slowly peeled away from the grove. It drifted over the trees and upward still. A silver outline of buildings upon the cloud flashed but disappeared as the cloud rose higher above Nantai.

Pristine silence remained.

Overhead, Selene shone brightly down upon Thalaj and me from a cloudless, starry sky.

DRAMATIS PERSONAE

Storm Sorcerers

Evangales and family

Atheryn Evangale—Tennō of Nantai; father to Karynne, Mairynne, and Yasmynne

Corwyn Dawnsgale—Nadia's consort, Solarynne's brother

Karynne "Kahry" Evangale—first daughter to Atheryn and Noralynne; Mairynne and Yasmynne's sister.

Mairynne Evangale—Lady Mairynne; third daughter to Atheryn and Noralynne

Nadialynne "Nadia" Riversgale—Noralynne's twin sister, aunt to Karynne, Mairynne, and Yasmynne

Noralynne Evangale—Kōgō of Nantai; empress; Atheryn's wife; mother to Karynne, Mairynne, and Yasmynne

Kōgō Phelyse—empress in the Second Age, second ruler of that age

Yasmynne Evangale—sister to Mairynne and Karynne; betrothed to Nestryn

First Advisors

Imrythel Sandsgale—Karynne's first advisor

Nestryn—Yasmynne's betrothed and first advisor

Clergy (raised to serve the Triad)

Arlyn Hallowgale—Priest of Otarr, the sun god/the Day-Seer

Baldwyn—Acolyte of Otarr, the sun god /the Day-Seer

Edamyn Hallowgale—Priest of Atun, the all-seeing god / the All-Seer; oldest priest

Tasmynne Hallowgale—Priestess of Selene, the moon goddess/the Night-Seer

Counselors

Azurynne Nightingale—matriarch of the Nightingale family

Lukosyn "Lukos" Thundergale—patriarch of the Thundergale family

Ohmyn Havengale—patriarch of the Havengale family

Solarynne Dawnsgale—Corwyn's sister, matriarch of the Dawnsgale family

Guards

Gaelynne

Roryn Seagale

Perryn

Tarlyn—leads the Arashi guard in Thalaj's absence

Thalaj Northerngale—Gensui of Nantai's Arashi guard

Other

Dorynne—Mairynne's attendant

Idalynne "Mother" Feathergale—nanny to Karynne, Mairynne, and Yasmynne

Jessamynne "Jessa" Feathergale—Idalynne's daughter,

friend to Mairynne

Larynne—Nadia's handmaid

Makenyn the Scarred—First Emperor of Nantai

Morwyn—Makenyn's brother

Nityn—Shaman who banished the dragon from Makenyn

Sentei **Summergale**—healer in Arashi

Teralynne - Healer apprentice

Zafrynne Keeningale—Witch woman/spellcaster

Deities (named) & Holy Triad

Holy Triad

Atun (aka the All-Seer)—Nantai God, part of the Holy Triad the all-seeing god; father to Otarr and Selene

Otarr (aka the Day-Seer)—Nantai God, part of the Holy Triad, associated with the sun; Atun's child; the sun god

Selene (aka the Night-Seer) —Nantai Goddess, part of the Triad, associated with the moon; Atun's daughter; the moon goddess

Ryū (Dragons, Ryū dragons, dragons)

Kuroidragon **(Kuroi)**, black dragon, bonded with Makenyn

Cloud Courtiers

Alto-Raal

Alto-Trea—The Swan

Cirro-Tsan—Comtess Tsanseri, Comtesse of the Masque; Lady of Masks

Cirro-Vior "Viordyn" —crescent moon shape on the shoulder; used to be a childhood friend of Mairynne's

Strato-Ymar—Gnoble of the caste

Fire Forgers

Yuos Atith—Gnoble of the caste

Frost Fighters (of the fourth caste)

Aljir Tenkara—Gnoble of the caste

Stone Singers

Sarangarel—Gnoble of the caste (female)

Underhill Dwellers

Brimr—Gnoble of the caste

Svarta—Brimr's wife